"I saved the best proposal of all for your ears only."

A streak of cold dread snaked downward. "You want a divorce, no doubt?"

At that he laughed, the sound engulfing her.

"Not a divorce, my lady wife, but an heir, and as you are the only woman who can legitimately give me one, the duty is all yours."

She almost tripped at his words and he held her closer, waiting until balance was regained. Their eyes locked. There was no humor at all in the green depths of Taylen Ellesmere, the sixth Duke of Alderworth.

He was deadly serious.

Shock gave her the courage to reply. "Then you have a large problem indeed, because I am the last woman in the world who would ever willingly grace your bed again."

* * *

The Dissolute Duke
Harlequin® Historical #1132—April 2013

Author Note

So many people have written to me and asked if I was going to write the story of Lucinda, the last sibling of the Wellinghams.

Well, here it is. Lucinda has featured in Asher's story, *High Seas to High Society,* Taris's story, *One Unashamed Night,* and Cristo's, *One Illicit Night.*

Falder has been like a second home to me for so many years—it is quite sad to have to say goodbye. I hope you love the way Lucinda's man is no pushover and, as the dissolute duke who has seemingly ruined their sister, is causing mayhem for the Wellingham brothers.

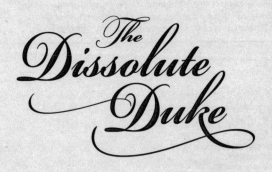

The Dissolute Duke

SOPHIA JAMES

HARLEQUIN® HISTORICAL

Recycling programs
for this product may
not exist in your area.

ISBN-13: 978-0-373-29732-0

THE DISSOLUTE DUKE

Copyright © 2013 by Sophia James

Printed in U.S.A.

Available from Harlequin® Historical and
SOPHIA JAMES

Fallen Angel #171
Ashblane's Lady #838
Masquerading Mistress #875
*High Seas to High Society #888
The Border Lord #946
Mistletoe Magic #973
*One Unashamed Night #1005
*One Illicit Night #1046
Gift-Wrapped Governess #1063
"Christmas at Blackhaven Castle"
Lady with the Devil's Scar #1102
*The Dissolute Duke #1132

*Linked by character

**Did you know some of these novels are also
available as ebooks? Visit www.Harlequin.com.**

I would like to dedicate this book to my sister-in-law, Susie.
Thanks for being a fan.

SOPHIA JAMES

Award-winning author Sophia James lives in New Zealand,
on Chelsea Bay on Auckland's North Shore with her husband,
who is an artist, and three children. She spends her morning
teaching adults English at the local migrant school and writes
in the afternoon. Sophia has a degree in English and history
from Auckland University and believes her love of writing
was formed reading Georgette Heyer with her twin sister at
her grandmother's house.

Chapter One

❧⤜⟩⟨⟩∞⟩⟨⟩⤛❧

England—1831

*H*er brothers would kill her for this.

Lady Lucinda Wellingham knew that they would.
Of all the hare-brained schemes that she had ever
been involved with, this was the most foolish of the
lot. She would be ruined and it would be entirely
her fault.

'Just a kiss,' the man whispered, pressing her
against a wall in the corridor, the smell of strong liquor on his breath. His hands wandered across the
line of her breasts, and in the ridiculously flimsy
dress that she had allowed Posy Tompkins to talk
her into wearing, Lucinda could feel where his next
thoughts lay.

Richard Allenby, third Earl of Halsey, had been
attractive at London society balls, but here at a country party in Bedfordshire he was intolerably cloying.

Pushing him away, she stood up straight, pleased that her height allowed her a good few inches above his own.

'I think, sir, that you have somehow got the wrong idea about my wish to…'

The words were cut off as his lips covered hers, a wet, limp kiss that made her turn her head away quickly before wiping her mouth. Goodness, the man was almost panting and it did not suit him at all.

'You are here at the most infamous party of the Season and my room isn't far.' His fingers closed across her forearm as he hailed two others who looked to have had as much to drink as he had. Both leered at her in the very same way that Halsey was. A mistake. She should have fled moments ago when the chance had been hers and the bedrooms had not been so perilously close. In this den of iniquity it seemed anything went, the morals of the man whose house it was fallen beyond all redemption.

A spike of fear brought her elbow against the wall, loosening Halsey's fingers and allowing a hard-won freedom which she took the chance on and ran.

Twisted and narrow corridors lay before her. There were close to twenty bedchambers on this floor alone and, moving quickly, Lucinda discovered double doors at the very end. With the corners she had taken she was certain those following would not see which door she had chanced upon and without a backward glance she turned an ornate ivory handle and slipped into the room.

It was dark inside save for a candle burning next to the bed, where a man sat reading, thick-rimmed glasses balanced on the end of his nose.

When he looked up she placed one finger to her lips, asking for his silence before turning back to the door. Outside she could hear the noise of those who followed her, the uncertainty of where she was adding to their urgency. Surely they would not dare to try their luck with any number of closed doors? A good few minutes passed, the whispers becoming less audible, and then they were gone, retracing their steps in the quest for the escaped quarry and ruing the loss of a night's entertainment. Relief filled her.

'Can I speak now?' The voice was laconic and deep, an inflection of something on the edge that Lucinda could not understand.

'If you are very quiet, I think it might be safe.' She looked around uncertainly.

A ripe swear word was her only answer and as the sheets were pushed back Lucinda saw the naked form of a man unfold from within them and her mouth gaped open. Not just any man either, but the scandalous host of this weekend's licentiousness: Taylen Ellesmere, the Sixth Duke of Alderworth. The Dissolute Duke, they called him, a rakehell who obeyed no laws of morality with his wanton disregard of any manners and his degenerate ways.

He was wearing absolutely nothing as he ambled across to the door behind her and locked it.

The sound seared into Lucinda's brain, but she found she could not even move a muscle.

He was beautiful. At least he was that, his dark hair falling to his shoulders and eyes the colour of wet leaves after a forest storm at Falder. She did not glance below the line of his neck, though every fibre of her being seemed to want her to. His smile said that he knew her thought, the creases around his eyes falling into humour.

'Lady Lucinda Wellingham?'

He knew her name. She nodded, trying to find her voice. What might happen next? She felt like a chicken in a fox's lair.

'Do your three brothers know that you are here?'

Her shake of the head was tempered by a lack of breath that indicated panic and she could barely take in air. Every single thing had gone wrong since dawn, so when her hands tried to open the stays of her bodice a little she was glad when they gave, allowing breath to come more easily. The deep false cleavage so desired by society women disappeared as the fasteners loosened, her breasts spilling back into their natural and fairly meagre form. The lurid red dress she wore fell away from the rise of her bosom in a particularly suggestive manner and she knew he observed it.

'Choosing my room to hide in might not have been the wisest of options.' He glanced tellingly towards the large bed.

Lucinda ignored the remark altogether. 'Richard

Allenby, the Earl of Halsey, and his friends gave me little other choice, your Grace. I had the need of a safe place.'

At that he laughed, the sound of mirth echoing about the chamber.

'Drink loosens the choking ties of societal pressure. Good manners and foppish decency is something most men cannot tolerate for more than a few weeks upon end and this place allows them to blow off steam, if you will.'

'At the expense of women who are saying no?'

'Most ladies here encourage such behaviour and dress accordingly.'

His eyes ran across the low-cut *décolletage* of her attire before returning to her face.

'This is not London, my lady, and nor does it pretend to be. If Halsey has indeed insulted you, he would have done so because he thought you were... available. Free will is a concept I set great store by here at Alderworth.'

The challenge in his eyes was unrepentant. Indeed, were she to describe his features she would say a measured indolence sat across them, like a lizard playing with a fly whose wings had already been disposed of. Her fingers went back to the door handle, but, looking for the key, she saw it had been removed. A quick sleight of hand. She had not seen him do it.

'As free will is so important to you, I would now

like to exercise my own and ask you to open the door.'

He simply leaned over to a pile of clothes roughly deposited on a chair and hauled out a fob watch.

'Unfortunately it is that strange time of the evening: too early for guests to be properly drunk and therefore harmless and too late to expect the conduct of gentlemen to be above reproach. Any movement through the house at this point is more dangerous than remaining here with me.'

'Remaining in here?' Could he possibly mean what she thought he did?

His eyes lightened. 'I have room.'

'You have known me for two minutes and half of those have been conducted in silence.' She tried to insert as much authority as she could into her announcement.

'All the better to observe your...many charms.' His green eyes were hooded with a sensual and languorous invitation.

'You sound like the wolf from the Grimm brothers' fairy tales, your Grace, though I doubt any character from a nursery rhyme exhibits the flair for nudity that you seem to display.'

Moving back from him, she was pleased when he pulled on a long white shirt, the sleeves billowing into wide folds from the shoulder. A garment a pirate might have worn or a highwayman. It suited him entirely.

'Is that better, my lady?'

When she nodded he smiled and lifted two glasses from a cabinet behind him. 'Perhaps good wine might loosen your inhibitions.'

'It certainly will not.' Her voice sounded strict even to her own ears and her eyes went to the book deposited on the counterpane. 'Machiavelli's *Il Principe* is a surprising choice for a man who seems to have no care for the name of the generations of Ellesmeres who have come before him.'

'You think all miscreants should be illiterate?'

Amazingly she began to laugh, so ridiculous was this conversation. 'Well, they are not usually tucked up in bed at ten o'clock wearing nothing but a pair of strong spectacles and reading a book of political philosophy in Italian, your Grace.'

'Believe me, degeneracy has a certain exhausting quality to it. The expectations for even greater acts of debauchery can be rather wearisome when age creeps up on one.'

'How old are you?'

'Twenty-five. But I have been at it for a while.'

He was only a year older than she was and her few public scrapes had always been torturous. Still he was a man, she reasoned, though the double standards of behaviour excusing his sex did not even come close to exonerating his numerous and shocking depravities.

'Did your mother not teach you the basics of human kindness to others, your Grace?'

'Oh, indeed she did. One husband and six lovers

later I understood it exactly. I was her only child, you see, and a very fast learner.'

She had heard the sordid story of the Ellesmere family many times, but not from the angle of a disenchanted son. Patricia Ellesmere had died far from her kin. There were those who said a broken heart had caused her death, but six lovers sounded particularly messy.

'What happened to your father?' She knew she should not have asked, but interest overcame any sense of reticence.

'He did what any self-respecting Duke might have done on discovering that his wife had cuckolded him six times over.'

'He killed himself?'

He laughed. 'No. He gambled away his fortune and then lost his woes in strong brandy. My parents died within a day of the other, at different ends of the country, and in the company of their newest lovers. Liver failure and a self-inflicted shot through the head. At least it made the funeral sum less expensive. Two for the price of one cuts the costs considerably.' His lips curled around the words and his green eyes were sharp. 'I was eleven at the time.'

Such candour was astonishing. No one had ever spoken to her like this before, a lack of apology in every new and dreadful thing he uttered.

Her own problems paled into insignificance at the magnitude of his and she could only be thankful for her close and supportive family ties.

'You had other relatives…to help you?'

'Mary Shields, my grandmother, took me in.'

'Lady Shields?' My God, who in society did not know of her proclivity for gossip and meanness? She had been dead for three years now, but Lucinda still remembered her beady black eyes and her vitriolic proclamations. And this was the woman whom an orphan child had been dispatched to?

'I see by your expression that you knew her?' He upended his tumbler and poured himself another. A generous another.

He wore rings on every finger on his left hand, she noticed, garish rings save for the band on his middle finger which was embellished with an engraving. She could not quite make out the letters.

A woman, no doubt. He was rumoured to have had many a lover, old and young, large and thin, married and unmarried. *He does not make distinction when appetite pounces.* She remembered hearing a rumour saying exactly that as it swirled around in society—a diverting scandal with the main player showing no sense of remorse.

The Duke of Alderworth. She knew that most of the ladies in society watched him, many a beating heart hoping that she might be the one to change him, but with his having reached twenty-five Lucinda doubted he would reform for anyone.

Foolish fancies were the prerogative of inexperienced girls. As the youngest sister of three rambunctious and larger-than-life brothers she found herself immune to the wiles of the opposite sex and seldom entertained any romantic notions about them.

Surprisingly, the lengthening silence between them was not awkward. That astonishing fact was made even more so by the thought that had he pushed himself upon her like Richard Allenby, the Earl of Halsey, she might have been quite pleased to see the result. But he did not advance on her in any way. Outside the screams of delight permeated this end of the corridor again, women's laughing shouts mingled with the deeper tone of their drunken pursuers. A hunting horn also blasted close, the loudness of it making her jump.

'A successful night, by the sounds. The hunters and the hunted in the pursuit of ecstasy. Soon enough there will be the silence of the damned.' He watched her carefully.

'I think you are baiting me, your Grace. I do not think you can be half as bad as they say you are.'

His expression changed completely.

'In that you would be very wrong, Lady Lucinda, for I am all that they say of me and more.' A new danger cloaked him, a hard implacability in his eyes that made him look older. 'The fact is that I could have you in my bed in a trice and you would be begging me not to stop doing any of the tantalising things to your body that I might want to.'

The pure punch of his words had her heart pounding fast, because in such a boast lay a good measure of truth. She was more aware of him as a man than she had ever been of any other. Horrified, Lucinda turned to the window and made much of looking out into the gardens, lit tonight by a number of burning torches positioned along various pathways. Two lovers lay entwined amidst the bushes, bare skin pale in the light. Around them other couples lingered, their intentions visible even from this distance. The intemperance of it all shocked her to the core.

'If you touch me, my brothers would kill you, most probably.' She attempted to keep fear from the threat and failed.

He laughed. 'They could try, I suppose, but...' The rest was left unsaid, but the menace in him was magnified. The indolence that she imagined before was now honed into cold hard steel, a man who existed in the underbelly of London's society even though he was high born. The contradictions in him confused her, the quicksilver change unnerving.

'I came to the party with Lady Posy Tompkins and she assured me that it was a respectable affair. Obviously she and I share a completely different idea of the word "respectable" and I suppose I should have made more of asking exactly where we were going before I said yes, but she was most insistent about the fun we might have and the fact that her godmother was coming made it sound more than respectable...'

He stopped her by laying his finger across the movement of her mouth. 'Do you always talk so much, Lady Lucinda?'

Her whole body jerked in response to the touch. 'I

do, your Grace, because when I am nervous I seem to be unable to stop although I don't quite remember another occasion when I have been as nervous as I am right at this moment, so if you were to let me walk from this room this instant I should go gladly and find—'

His mouth came to the place where his finger had lingered, and Lucinda's world dissolved into hot colourful fragments of itself, tipping any sense of reality on its head and replacing ordinariness with a dangerous molten pleasure.

Chapter Two

Tay just wanted her to stop talking, the edge of panic in her voice bringing forth a guilt that he hadn't felt for years. The slight curve of her breasts fitted into his chest and he liked the softness. Usually he had to bend down to women, but this one stood only a few inches below him, her thinness accentuating her willowy figure in an almost boyish way.

Her nails were short and the calluses between her second and third fingers told him she was left handed and that she participated in some sort of sport. Archery, perhaps. The thought of her standing, aiming at a target and her blonde hair lifting in the breeze was strangely arousing. He should, of course, escort her from Alderworth post-haste and make certain that she was delivered home safely into the bosom of her family.

But he knew that he would not, and when he took her mouth against his, another feeling surfaced which he refused to dwell on altogether.

He did not imagine she had been kissed much before because her full lips were held in a tight line and, as he opened her mouth with his tongue, her eyes widened.

Eyes of pale blue etched with a darker shade—eyes a man could lose himself in completely and never recover from.

Softening his assault, he threaded his hands through her hair, tilting her face. This time he did not hurry or demand more as the heat of a slow burn built. God, she smelt so good, like the flowers in an early springtime, fresh and clean. He had become so used to the heady over-ripe perfumes of his many experienced *amours* that he had forgotten the difference.

Innocence. It smelt strangely like hope.

Sealing his mouth across hers, he brought his fingers behind her nape. Closer. Warmer.

The power of connection winded him, the first tentative exploration of her tongue poignant in a way that made him melancholy. It had been a long time since he had kissed a woman who watched him as if he might unlock the secrets of the universe.

Lust ignited, an incendiary living torch of need burning bright, like the wick of gunpowder snaking down through his being. Unstoppable.

'Are you a virgin?'

He knew she was by the way she was breathing, barely enough air to fill her up, lost in the moment and her lips parted. 'Yes.'

'Why the hell did you come to this party, then?' The layer of civilisation that he had tried to keep in place was gone with the feel of her, but there was no withdrawal as he asked the question. Rather she pressed in closer and shut her eyes, as though trying in the darkness to find an answer. He felt the feathery waft of her breath in the sensitive folds of his neck and wondered if she was quite as innocent as he presumed. If this was a game she played, then it was one that he had long been practised in and she would need to be careful. His hands went around her back of their own accord, like a pathway memorised.

Salvation.

The word came unbidden and blossomed into something that he could not deny and his pulse began to quicken. It had been years since he had felt like this with any woman and surprise spurred him onwards.

He twisted her and his mouth fell lower, laving at the skin at her neck, his attention bringing whorls of redness to the pale. Her breath matched his own now, neither quiet nor measured, for the power of the body had taken over and his thumb caressed the budding hardness of one nipple through crimson silk.

She arched back, thighs locked tight, her breasts twin beacons of temptation.

He wanted her as he had never wanted another in all his life, the feel of her, the softness, her hair light-spun gold against his dark. With a small motion he had her bodice loosened and his palm around the bounty of one breast, cupping flesh, stroking the firmness. He needed her devoid of clothing, wanting pure knowledge without a covering. If she had not been the lady he knew she was, he would have simply ripped the garment off from neckline to hemline, and transported her naked to his bed to take his fill. His mouth ached for the intimacy of her curves.

'The taste of a lover is part of the attraction,' he stated simply as he raised his head, watching as understanding dawned. Uncertainty chased on the heels of wariness, but still she did not pull away as he thought she might. Only a slight frown marred her brow, measuring intent without any fear whatsoever. A guileless allowance.

Such an emotion was something he had rarely experienced. His reputation had protected him, he supposed, and kept others at a distance. But Lucinda Wellingham was different and more dangerous than all of the sirens who had stalked him across so many years. The connection between them was unexpected and startling as it drew him in, his body tightening in the echo of an old knowledge. His head dipped and he brought one soft peak into his mouth, the force of the action ripping stretched red silk and the seam shirring into uncountable and damaged threads. He liked the way she arched into him, her fingers combing through his hair, nails hard-edged with want, taking his offering and giving him back her own.

His hands now moved from the rise of her bottom around the front to feel for the hidden folds of womanhood, the silk only a thin barrier to taking. He pressed in to find her centre.

'No.' A single word, moaned more than stated, but enough.

'No?' He had to make certain that that was what she had meant, his breath coming thick with need. She shook her head this time, sky-blue eyes devoid of everything, a frown on her forehead and her chest rising and falling.

No, because she could not envisage what a yes might mean? No, because he was a man with enough of a reputation to destroy her?

Breaking away he moved back, the anger in him mounting with a pounding awareness of guilt. The road to ruin was a short one and he knew a lady of her ilk would have no possible defence against his persuasions. Suddenly his own chosen life path seemed seedy and vulgar.

'I will take you home.'

She did not repair the damage to her dress as she watched him so that one breast stood out naked from the loosened fabric, a pink-rosebud nipple beckoning against scarlet silk. With her glassy eyes and stillness she was like a sensual and pliant Madonna fallen from heaven to land at the feet of the devil. Indecision welled, but he had no shield against such goodness, no way to safeguard his yearning against her righteousness.

Stepping forwards, he readjusted her gown, retying the laces on the flimsy bodice so that some measure of decency was reinstated. He could do nothing to repair the ruined seam and his eyes were drawn to the show of flesh that curved outwards beneath it, calling for his attentions. Swearing, he took a blanket from his bed and laid it around her, the wool almost the same shade as her hair. Then he collected his clothes, pulling on his breeches and placing a jacket over the shirt. He did not stop for a cravat. His boots were shoved on stockingless feet at the door as he retrieved the key and unlocked it.

'Come, sweetheart,' he murmured and found her hand, liking the way her slender fingers curled around his own.

Trust.

Another barrier breached. He yearned for others.

Outside it was quiet and, as the stables materialised before them, a lad came to his side.

'Ye'd be wanting the carriage at this time of the night, your Grace?' Disbelief was evident in the query. Normally conveyances were not sent for until well into the noon hours of the next day. Or the one after that.

'Indeed. Find Stephens and have it readied. I need to go to London.'

When the boy left them Lucinda Wellingham began to speak, her voice low and uncertain. 'My cloak is still in the house and my hat and reticule. Should I not get them?'

'No.' Tay wanted only to be gone. He had no idea

who would talk about her appearance at one of the most infamous and least salubrious parties of the Season, but if he had her home at the Wellingham town house before the morning surely her brothers would be able to fashion a story which would dispel all rumour.

'My friend Posy Tompkins might wonder what has happened to me. I hope that she is safe.' She did not meet his eyes at all, a contrite Venus who had tripped into the underworld unbidden and now only wanted to be released from it.

'Safe?' He could not help laughing, though the sound was anything but humorous. 'No one at my parties is safe. It is generally their singular intention not to be.'

'Enjoying herself, then?' she countered without missing a beat, the damn dimples in her cheeks another timely reminder of her innate goodness.

'Oh, I can almost swear that she will be that. The thrall of a good orgasm is highly conducive to contentment.'

Silence reigned, but he had to let her know. Who he was. What he was. Her muteness heartened him.

'I am not safe, Lady Lucinda, and neither am I repentant. When you came to Alderworth dressed in the sort of gown that raises dark fantasies in the minds of any red-blooded man, surely you understood at least that?'

Tears glittered and Tay swore, causing more again to pool beneath the light of the lamp.

'Lord knows, you are far too sweet for a sinner like me and tomorrow you will realise exactly just how close to ruin you were and be thankful that I took you home, no matter the loss of a few possessions.'

Asher, Taris and Cristo would not have called her sweet. Not in a million years. She was a failure and a liability to the Wellingham name and she always had been. That was the trouble. She was 'intrinsically flawed'. The gypsy who had read her palm in a stall outside the Leadenhall Market had looked directly into her eyes and told her so.

Intrinsically flawed.

And she was. Tonight was living proof of the ridiculous things she did, without thought for responsibility or consequence. With a little less luck she could have been in the Duke of Alderworth's bed right now, knees up around his bare and muscled thighs and knowing what a great many of the less principled women of English society already did. It was only his good sense that had stopped her, for she had been far beyond putting a halt to anything. With just a little persuasion she would have followed him to his bed in the candlelight. Shame coated her, the thick ignominy making her feel ill. Such a narrow escape.

An older man came towards them, carrying a light, and behind him again a whole plethora of busy servants. Lucinda did not meet their eyes as they observed her, plastering a look on her face that might pass for indifference. Goodness, how she hoped that there was none amongst these servants of Alderworth who might have a channel of communication into the empire of the Wellinghams.

At her side Alderworth made her feel both excited and nervous, his heat calling her to him in a way that scorched sense. When his arm came against her own she did not pull away, the feel of him exciting and forbidden before he moved back. She took in one deep breath and then let it out slowly, trying to find logic and reason and failing.

His gaze swept across her with all the intensity of a ranging and predatory tiger.

Within moments the conveyance was ready to leave, the lamps lit and the driver in place. Without touching her Taylen Ellesmere indicated that she climb up and when she sat on a plush leather seat, he chose the opposite side to rest on, his green eyes brittle.

'It will take us four hours to reach Mayfair. If you are still cold…?'

'No, I am fine.' She pulled the blanket further about her, liking the shelter.

'Good.' Short and harsh.

Glancing out of the window, she saw in the faded reflection her stricken and uncertain face.

What did the Duke of Alderworth make of her? Was he as irritated by her uncertainty as he was with her intemperance? She could sense he wanted her gone just as soon as he could get her there, a woman who had strayed unbidden into a place she had no reason to be in; a woman who did not play the games that he was so infamous for.

Why he should hoist himself into the carriage in the first place was a mystery. He looked like a man who would wish to be anywhere but opposite her in a small moving space.

It was the kiss, probably, and the fact that she did not know quite how to kiss a man back. Her denial of anything more between them would have also rankled, an innocent who had played with fire and had burnt them both because of it. Granted, two or three forward beaux had planted their lips on her mouth across the years, but the offerings had always been chaste and tepid and nothing like…

No, she would not think about that. Taylen Ellesmere was a fast-living and dissolute rake who would be far from attracted to the daughter of one of London's most respectable families. He had all the women he wanted, after all, loose women, beautiful women, and she had heard it said time after time that he did not wish to be shackled by the permanency of marriage.

She shook her head hard and listened to what he was saying now.

'I shall deny that you were at Alderworth tonight should I be questioned about it. Instruct your brothers to do the same.'

'They might not need to know anything if I am lucky…'

'It is my experience that scandal does not exist in the same breath as luck, Lucinda.'

A strange warmth infused her as he said her name. She had never really liked 'Lucinda' much, but when he pronounced it he made it sound…sensual. The timbre of some other promise lay on the edge of his words.

'Believe me, with good management any damage can be minimised.'

Damage. Reality flared. She was only a situation to be managed. The night crawled in about them, small shafts of moonlight illuminating the interior of the coach. Outside the rain had begun to fall heavily, a sudden shower in a windless night.

Taylen Ellesmere was exactly like her brothers, a man who liked control and power over everything about him. No surprises or unwanted quandaries. The thought made her frown.

'I do not envisage problems,' he said. 'If you play your part well, there should not be—'

A shout split the air, and then the carriage simply rolled to one side further and further, the wild scrunch of metal upon wood and a jerking lurch.

Leaping over beside her, the Duke braced her in his arms, protecting her from the splintering glass as it shattered inwards, a cushion against the rocking chaos and the rush of cold air. He held her so tightly she felt the punching hardness of metal on his body, drawing blood and making him grimace.

Then there was only darkness.

Lucinda was in her own room at Falder House in Mayfair, the curtains billowing in a quiet afternoon breeze, the sounds of the wind in the trees and further off in the park the voices of children calling.

Everything exactly normal save for her three sisters-in-law dressed in sombre shades and sitting in a row of chairs watching her.

'You are awake?'

Beatrice-Maude came forwards and lifted Lucinda's head carefully before offering a sip of cold lemonade that sat in a glass on the bedside table. 'The doctor said he thought you would return to us today and he was right.' She smiled as she carefully blotted any trace of moisture from Lucinda's lips. 'How do you feel?'

'How should I feel?'

Something was not right. Some quiet and creeping thing was being hidden from her, crouched in the shadows of truth.

'Why am I here? What happened?'

'You don't remember?' Emerald now joined Beatrice-Maude and her face was solemn. 'You don't remember an accident, Lucy?'

'Where?' Panic had begun to consume her and she tried to sit up, but nothing seemed to work, her arms, her legs, her back. All numb and useless. The feel of her heart pumping in her chest was the only thing that still functioned and she felt light headed at the fear of paralysis.

'I cannot move.'

'Doctor Cameron said that was a normal thing. He said many people regain the use of their bodies after the swelling has subsided.'

'Swelling?'

'You suffered a blow to the neck and a nasty bang on the head. It was lucky that the coach to Leicester was passing by the other way, because otherwise...'

'You could have been there all night and Doctor Cameron said you may not have lived.' Eleanor, her youngest brother's wife, had joined in now, but unlike the others her voice shook and her face was blotchy. She had been crying. A lot.

This realisation frightened Lucinda more than anything else had.

'How did it happen?'

'Your carriage overturned. There was a corner, it seems, and the vehicle was moving too fast. It plummeted down a hill a good many yards and came to rest at the bottom of the incline.'

Agitation made her shake as more and more words tumbled into the chasm of blankness her brain had become.

Beatrice took over, holding her hand tightly, and managing a forced smile. 'It is over now, sweetheart. You are home and you are safe and that is all that is important.'

'How did I get here?'

'Asher brought you back three days ago.'

Lucinda swallowed. Three days. Her mind tried its hardest to find any recollection of the passage of time and failed.

And now she was cast upon this bed as a figure of stone, her head and heart the only parts of her body that she could still feel. A tear leaked its way from her left eye and fell warm down her cheek into the line of her hair. Swallowing, her throat thick and raw, she had the taste of blood on her tongue.

Screaming. A flash of sound came back through the ether. *Screaming and screaming. Her voice and another calming her. Quiet and sad, warm hands holding her neck so that she did not move, the night air cold and wet and the rain joining blood.*

'Doctor Cameron said it was a miracle you did not move another inch as you would have been dead. He says it was fortunate that when they found you, your head had been stabilised between two heavy planks of wood to restrain any motion.'

'Lucky,' she countered, the sentiment falling into question.

They were not telling her the whole of it. She could see it in the shared looks and feel it in the hushed unspoken reticence. She wondered why her brothers were not here in the room and knew the answer to the question as soon as she thought it.

They would not be able to hide things from her as

easily as her sisters-in-law, although Cristo was still most efficient at keeping his own council.

'Was anyone else hurt?'

The hesitation told her there had been.

'There was a man in the carriage with you, Lucy.' Emerald now took her other hand, rubbing at it in a way that was supposed to be comforting, she supposed, though it felt vaguely annoying because her skin was so numb.

'I was alone with him?' Nothing made sense. What could she have been doing on the open road at night and in the company of a stranger? It was all too odd. 'Who was he?'

'The sixth Duke of Alderworth.' Beatrice took up the story now.

'Alderworth?' Lucinda knew the name despite not remembering anything at all about the accident.

My God. The Dissolute Duke was infamous across London and it seemed he kept to the company of whores and harpies almost exclusively. Why would she have been there alone with him and so far from home?

'Does Asher know he was there?' She looked up at Emerald.

'Unfortunately he does.'

'Do other people also know?

'Unfortunately they do.'

'How many know?'

'All of London would not be putting too fine a point on it, I think.'

'I see. It is a scandal then and I am ruined?'

'No.' Beatrice-Maude's voice was strong. 'Your brothers would never allow that to happen and neither will we.'

Lucinda swallowed, the whole conundrum more than she could deal with. Eleanor and Emerald watched her with a certain worry in their eyes and even Beatrice, who was seldom flustered, seemed out of sorts.

Intrinsically flawed. The words came from nowhere as she closed her eyes and slept.

Chapter Three

T ay Ellesmere sat in the library of the Carisbrook family town house in Mayfair and looked at the three Wellingham brothers opposite him.

His head ached, his right leg was swollen above the knee and the top of his left arm was encased in a heavy white bandage, as were his ribs, strapped tightly so that breathing was not quite so agonising. Besides this he had myriad other cuts and grazes from the glass and wood splintering as the carriage had overturned.

But these injuries were the very least of his worries. A far more pressing matter lingered in the air between him and his hosts.

'You were dressed most inappropriately and Lucinda was barely dressed at all, for God's sake. The scandal is the talk of the town and has been for the past week.'

Asher Wellingham, Duke of Carisbrook, seldom minced words and Tay did not dissemble, either.

'Our lack of clothing was the result of being thrown over and over down a hill in a somersaulting carriage. One does not generally emerge from such a mishap faultlessly attired,' he drawled the reply, knowing that it would annoy them, but short of verifying their sister's presence at his party he could do little else but blame the accident.

'We thought Lucinda had gone with Lady Posy Tompkins to her aunt's country home for the weekend. I cannot for the life of me imagine how instead she ended up alone in the middle of the night with the most dissolute Duke in all of London town and dressed as a harpy.'

'Did you ask her?'

'She can remember nothing.' Taris Wellingham broke in now, his stillness as menacing as his older brother's fury.

'Nothing?'

'Nothing before the accident, nothing during the accident and nothing just after the accident.'

Hope flared. Perhaps it might give him an escape after all. If the lady was not baying for his blood, then her brothers might also give up the chase should he play his cards well.

'Your sister informed me that she was trying to reach the Wellingham town house after being separated somehow from her friend. She merely asked me to give her a lift home and I immediately assented.'

'Her reticule, hat and cloak were returned to us from your country seat. A coincidence, would you not say, to be left at the very place you swear she was not.'

Cristo Wellingham's voice sounded as flat as his brothers'.

'Richard Allenby, the Earl of Halsey, has also told half of London that she was a guest at your weekend soirée. Others verify his story.'

'He lies. I was the host and your sister was not there.'

'The problem is, Duke, Lucinda is facing certain ruin and you do not seem to be taking your part in her downfall seriously.'

Taylen had had enough.

'Ruin is a strong word, Lord Taris.'

'As strong as retribution.'

Asher Wellingham's hand hit the table and Tay stood. Even with his arm in a bandage he could give the three of them a good run for their money. The art of gentlemanly fighting had been a lesson missing from his life, the tough school of displacement and abuse honing the rudiments of the craft instead. Hell, he had been beaten enough himself to understand exactly the best places to hit back.

'We will kill you for this, Alderworth, I swear that we will.' Cristo spoke now, the sound of each word carefully enunciated.

'And in doing so you may well crucify your sister. Better to let the matter rest, laugh it off and kick any suggestions of misbehaviour back in the face of those who swear them true.'

'As you are apt to do?'

'English society still holds to ridiculously strict rules of conduct, though free speech is finding its way into the minds of men who would do better to believe in it.'

'Men like you?' Taris stood. His reported lack of sight was not apparent as he stepped towards the window, though Tay saw the oldest brother watch him carefully.

Care.

The word reverberated inside him. This was what this was all about, after all: care of each other, care of a family name, care in protecting their only sister's reputation from the ignominy of being linked with his.

Protection was something he himself had never had. Not from his parents. Not from his grandmother. And particularly not from his uncle. It had always been him against a world that hadn't taken the time to make sure that a small child was cherished. The man he had become was the result of such negligence, though here in the salon of a family that watched each other's backs the thought was disheartening.

He made his way around a generous sofa. 'I have an errand to attend to, gentlemen, and I find I have the need of some fresh air. If you will excuse me.'

* * *

'What do you make of him?'

Asher asked the question a few moments later as Cristo crossed to the cabinet to pull out a bottle of fine French brandy.

'He's hiding something.' Taris accepted a drink from his brother. 'For some reason he is trying to make us believe there was only necessity in our sister's foolish midnight tryst in the carriage with him and that she was never at Alderworth.'

Cristo swore. 'But why would he do that?'

'Even a reprobate must have his limits of depravity, I suppose. Lucinda's innocence may well be his.' Taris drank deeply of the brandy before continuing. 'He studies the philosophy of the new consciousness, which is interesting, the tenets of free speech being mooted in the Americas. Unusual reading for a man who purports to be interested in nothing more than sexual mayhem and societal anarchy.'

'I don't trust him.' Asher upended his glass.

'Well, we can't hit a man wrapped in bandages.' Cristo smiled.

'Then we wait until they are removed.' There was no humour at all in the voice of Asher Wellingham, Duke of Carisbrook.

Lucinda wheeled herself to the breakfast table, her muscles straining against the task and her heart pounding with the effort. It had been almost two weeks since the accident and the feeling that the doctor had sworn she would recover was finally coming back, though she had been left with a weakness that felt exhausting and a strange and haunting melancholy. Now she could walk for short distances without falling over, the shaking she had been plagued by diminishing as she grew steadily in strength. The wheelchair was, however, still her main mode of getting about.

Posy had spent much of the past week at the town house, her horror at all that had happened to Lucy threading every sentence.

'I should never have taken you to Alderworth, Luce. It is all my fault this happened to you and now…now I don't know how to make it better.' Large tears had fallen down her cheeks before tracing wet runnels on the pink silk of her bodice.

'You did not force me to go, Posy. I remember that much.'

'But while I was safely locked away in our bedroom, you were…'

'Let's not allocate any more blame. What is done is done and at least I am regaining movement and energy.'

It had taken Lucinda a good few days to convince her friend that she held no malice or blame, Posy's numerous tears a wearying and frustrating constant.

Asher was sitting in the dining room, reading *The Times* just as he usually did each morning, and he folded the paper in half and looked closer as something caught his interest.

'It says here that the Earl of Halsey has suffered a broken nose, a black eye and twenty stitches in his cheek. The assault happened in broad daylight four days ago in an altercation outside the livery stables in Davies Mews right here in Mayfair. There were no witnesses.'

His glance strayed to Lucinda's to see how she might react. The whole family had tiptoed around her since the *unfortunate happening* as though she might break into pieces at any unwanted reminder of scandal and she was tired of it. Consequently she did nothing more than smile back at her oldest brother and shrug her shoulders.

'Footpads are becoming increasingly confident, then.' Emerald took up the conversation as she buttered her bread. 'Though perhaps they do us a favour, for isn't he the man who has constantly insisted Lucinda was underdressed at the Alderworth fiasco? Without his voice, all of this could have been so much easier to deal with.'

Lucinda knew Richard Allenby, of course. He had always been well mannered and rather sweet, truth be told, so she had no idea why he should be maligning her now and in such a fashion. Yet a shadow lingered there in the very back of her mind, some nebulous and half-formed thing trying to escape from the darkness. Wiping her mouth with the napkin, she sat back, the food suddenly dry in her mouth and difficult to swallow.

'You look like you have seen a ghost, Lucy.'

'What exactly was it that the Earl of Halsey said of me?'

'He has been spreading the rumour that you may have been intimate with Alderworth at his home. He says he saw you in the corridors on the first floor of the place, searching for the host's bedchamber.'

Her brother's tone had that streak of exasperation she so often heard when speaking of her escapades, though in this case Lucinda could well understand it.

'Intimate?' The shock of such a blatant falsehood was horrifying. 'Why would he tell such a lie? Surely people could not believe him?' Wriggling her foot against the metal bar of the wheelchair, she checked for any further movement. Over the past few days the tingling had gone from her knees to her feet as the numbness receded.

'Unfortunately they are beginning to.' Asher's voice no longer held any measure of care.

'What does Alderworth say?'

'Nothing and that is the great problem. If he denied everything categorically and strode into society the same way he strode into Wellingham House, people might cease to believe Richard Allenby. But instead the man has disappeared to the country, leaving chaos behind him.'

'Alderworth came here? To the town house?' Lucinda frowned. There was something about him that was familiar, some part of him that she remembered from…before. 'What did he want?'

'Put bluntly, he wanted to be rid of any blame

as far as your reputation was concerned. He made that point very plain.' Asher put his paper down and watched her closely. 'The man is a charlatan, but he is also clever. The slight whiff of an alliance with us might be profitable to him.'

'Alliance?' Lucinda's mouth felt suddenly dry.

'A ruined reputation requires measures that may be stringent and far from temporary.'

'You mean a betrothal?' Horror had Lucinda's words whispered. Low. She had heard all the stories of the wicked Duke. Everybody had. He was a man who lived by his own rules and threw the caution most others followed to the wind.

As her heartbeat quickened, memory fought against haze and won. Dropping the teacup she was holding, she stood, liquid spilling across the pristine whiteness of an antique damask tablecloth, the brown stain widening through the embossed stitching even as she watched.

The naked form of Taylen Ellesmere came through the fog, unfolding from a rumpled bed, each long and graceful line etched in candlelight, the red wine in a decanter beside him almost gone. She knew the feel of his skin, undeniably, for they had been joined together pressed in lust, his velvet-green eyes close as he had leaned down and kissed her. No simple chaste kiss, either, but one with a smouldering and virtue-taking force.

Shock kept her still, as she looked directly at her oldest brother.

'What is wrong? You look…ill.' Real concern crossed his face.

'I am remembering things and I th-th-think everything Richard Halsey is saying of m-me might indeed be tr-true.'

Her weakened legs folded beneath her just as Asher caught her, the hard arm of the chair slamming into her side.

'You are saying you lay with Alderworth. Unmarried.'

'He was naked in his bedchamber. He touched me everywhere. The door was locked and I could not leave. I tried to, but I could not. He took the key. He was not safe.' A torrent of small truths, each one worse than the last.

'My God.' She had never heard the note in her brother's voice that she did now, not once in all her many escapades and follies. His fractured tone brought tears to her eyes as she felt Emerald's hand slip into her own and squeeze.

'You will marry my sister as soon as I can procure a special licence and then you will disappear from England altogether, you swine.'

Asher Wellingham had already laid a good few punches across Tay's face and Cristo Wellingham was still holding him down. Not the refined manners he had imagined them to have, after all, each blow given with a deliberate and clinical precision. His nose streamed with blood and he could barely see out of his left eye. The two front teeth at the bottom of his mouth were loosened.

'If you kill me…a betrothal might be…difficult.'

Another blow caught him in the kidneys and, despite meaning not to, he winced.

'You will tell Lucinda that it was completely your fault she was at Alderworth in the first place and that your heinous, iniquitous and pernicious sense of social virtue was lost years before you met her. In effect, you will say that she never had the chance of escaping such corruption.'

'C-comprehensive.'

'Very. But as long as you understand us we will allow you to at least take breath into another day whilst we try to mitigate all the wrong you have heaped upon our sister. She is distraught, as you can well imagine, and names you as the most loathsome of all men. A reprobate who took advantage of her when she was drunk.'

'She told you that?'

'And worse. But although she might hate you, she also knows that you are the only man who can restore her shattered name in society when you marry her. In that she is most adamant.'

'A sterling quality in a bride.' Even to his own ears his voice lacked the sting of irony he usually made an art form of.

'Well, you can laugh, Alderworth, but if you believe we will let you anywhere near Lucinda after the ceremony is performed then you have another think coming. You have already done your damage. Now you will pay for it.'

Tay coughed once and then again, his breath difficult to catch. When the younger brother allowed him to drop heavily to the floor he felt the arm that had been hurt in the carriage accident crack against hard parquet, pain radiating up into the shoulder socket.

Ignominiously he began to shake and he swore. It had been a long time since he remembered doing that, his uncle's face screwed up above him in the wrath of some perceived and tiny insult, the summer winds of Alderworth hot against the wounds that lashed his back. Bleeding, everywhere. No mercy in the beating.

Standing uncertainly and holding on to the edge of a chair, he raised himself before them. 'Your sister's memory is faulty. I did not touch her.'

'She says exactly the opposite, and anybody who knows Lucinda knows, too, that straightforward honesty is one of her greatest strengths.' The embossed ducal ring on Carisbrook's finger caught the light as he moved forwards. 'Frankly, given the number of your dubious guests who have not ceased gossiping since the accident about what went on at Alderworth, I find your whining and feeble excuses insulting. A man worth his salt would simply own up to his mistakes and take the punishment he deserves.'

From experience Tay knew when to stop baiting a man who would hit him until life was leached from truth. He nodded an end to the dispute and saw the answering relief on Asher Wellingham's face.

'We will pay you to leave a week after the wedding. A considerable sum that should see you well on your way to your next destination. After that, you will never again set foot anywhere near London or our family.'

'Alderworth is almost bankrupt. Your father's debts were numerous and you will not have enough equity to continue the repayments after the year's end.' Taris had taken up the reins now, from a sofa near the fireplace, his voice steady and quiet. 'You have been trying to trade your way out of the conundrum, but your bills are becoming onerous and a lifestyle of indolence is hardly a profitable one. Accept our offer and you might keep your family inheritance for a few years yet. Decline and you will be in the debtors' prison by Christmas.'

'Will your sister know?'

'Indeed. Lucinda wants it.' Cristo stepped forwards, disdain in his eyes. 'She wants you out of her life for ever.'

Marriage as a bribe to keep the Alderworth estate. Tay thought of its roofline under the Bedfordshire sky, the golden stone against the sun and hundreds of acres of fertile and green land at its feet. His father had forsaken the place, but he could not. Not even if the alternative meant selling his soul.

'Very well.' His voice was hoarse and he felt his honour breaking, but he swiped the feeling away as a quill was inked and a parchment made ready. He was the only Alderworth who could save four hundred years of history and Lucinda Wellingham hated his very guts.

Chapter Four

Lord Taylen Ellesmere, the sixth Duke of Alderworth, had the appearance of a man who had been in a particularly rough boxing match when Lucinda saw him for the first time at the top of the aisle in the small chapel in London's Mayfair.

He did not turn to look at her, his profile granite-hard, his left wrist encased in a bandage and a large cut running along the whole side of his jaw. The muscles beneath the wound rippled with anger, a barely held wrath that was seen in the straightness of his posture and in the rigidity of his being. His hair was shorter, shaved almost to the skull, a single white, opaque scar snaking from the edge of his right ear to his crown. One eye was blackened.

Even Asher looked slightly taken aback by his appearance, but at this stage of the proceedings there was little anyone could do.

The die was cast after all. She would marry the

Duke of Alderworth to redeem her place in society and he would marry her because her brothers had made him do so. She had sinned and this was the result. Love existed nowhere in the equation and the empty pews in the chapel reflected the fact. Her siblings and their wives sat on her side of the church, as well as some close friends, but on his side…there was nobody.

Lucinda speculated as to who might stand up as his witness, the question answered a moment later when Cristo moved across to him. Her youngest brother looked about as unhappy with the whole thing as Asher was, a duty performed out of necessity rather than respect.

Every other Wellingham wedding had been a joyous affair, celebrated with laughter and noise and elation. This one was sombre, quiet and dismal. She wondered how long the Duke of Alderworth would stay in London after the ceremony and just what words she might use to explain away his absence. Asher had said that he would remain in the capital for a week or more, so that appearances could be upheld. After that they would be glad to see the back of him.

Her brother had breathed this through a clenched jaw as if even a day in the company of her soon-to-be husband would be one too many.

Lucinda swallowed away dry fear. This was the worst mistake she had ever made, but the consequences of her own stupidity had brought her to such a pass, her whole family entwined in the deceit. She wanted to throw down the bouquet of white roses interlaced with fragrant gardenias and peel off the ivory gown that had been quickly fashioned by one of London's up-and-coming modistes. The veil helped, however, a layer of lace between her and the world, sheltering confusion. A week ago she would not have been able to walk or to stand for such long periods, but today the utter alarm of everything allowed her to keep any pain at bay.

Posy Tompkins stood to one side of her, her face drawn. Her friend had been nothing short of horrified about the consequences of their ill-thought-out visit to Alderworth and had been attentive and apologetic ever since. She claimed she had managed to avoid the worst of the excesses by locking herself in her room.

'Are you sure you want to go through with this, Luce?' she whispered. 'We could disappear to Europe together otherwise. I have more than enough money for us both. We could go to Rome or Paris to my relatives.'

'And be for ever outcast?'

'It might be better than…' She stopped, but Lucinda knew exactly what she was about to say.

It might be better than being married to a man who looked for all the world as if he was going to his own funeral. With an effort she lifted her chin. It was not as if she was happy about anything, either, although some quiet part of her buried deep held its breath as green eyes raked across her own, the red streak in one of them bright with fury.

'This is 1831, Luce, not the Middle Ages. If you truly do not wish to do this, you only have to say. No one can drag a reluctant bride to the altar even if the alternative is enormous scandal.'

'I do not think your words are helping, Posy.'

'Then let me call it off. I can say that it was completely my fault I took you to Alderworth in the first place and procured the dress and...'

But the minister had begun to speak in his low, calm voice and Lucinda knew that to simply walk out on her last chance of salvation would be to cut herself off from a family that meant the world to her.

She had brought this upon herself, after all, and she just could not think of another more viable solution. A marriage ceremony. A week of pretence. And then freedom. Lord, she would follow the straight and narrow from now on and, if God in all his wisdom allowed her the strength to get through these next hours, she would promise in return an eternal devotion to His Good Works.

When Tay took a quick look at his bride-to-be he saw that under her veil her hair was plaited in a crown encircled by pale rosebuds. Today she seemed smaller, slighter, less certain. The lies she had spun about them, he supposed, come home to roost in front of the altar, no true basis for any such betrothal. He was glad of the lace that covered her head because he did not wish to see her deceitful eyes until he had to. The gown surprised him, though. He had thought she might balk at making any effort whatsoever, but the dress fitted her perfectly, spilling in a froth of whiteness about her feet. A dainty silver bracelet adorned her left wrist, four small gold stars hanging from it.

A continual whispered dialogue with the bridesmaid began to get on his nerves and he was glad when the minister, dressed in flowing dark clothes, called the place to order.

Everybody looked tense. The bride. The brothers. Even the minister as he held his hand up to the organist and called for quiet.

'Marriage is a state that is not to be entered into lightly, or with false promise. Are you happy to continue, Lady Lucinda?'

Tay bit down on chagrin. Of course she would be. His title was one factor and her ruin was another. He wished the man might skip through to the final troths and then all of this would be over.

But he did not. Rather he waited until the bride before him nodded her head without any enthusiasm whatsoever. 'Then we are here today to join this man and this woman in the state of Holy Matrimony...'

For ever and for ever. It was all Tay could think as he gave his replies, though his parents had never let such pledges inhibit them in their quest for the hedonistic. For the first time in his life he partly understood them and some of his disillusionment lifted.

But it was too late for such understanding now,

with his years seemingly destined to run along the same chaotic and uncontrolled pathway as those that he had sworn he would never follow. He was his father's son, after all, and this was a universally ordained celestial punishment for what he had become. The thought calmed him; fate moving in ways which allowed no redemption and if it had not been this particular sticky end that he had met, then undoubtedly it would have been another.

'Will you, Taylen Andrew Templeton Ellesmere, take Lucinda Alice Wellingham as your lawfully wedded wife…?'

The words shook him from his reverie. Her middle name was Alice and it suited her. Soft. Pale. Otherworldly.

'I will.'

Resignation tempered his pledge.

When Lucinda Wellingham gave the troth her tone was shaken, a thin voice in a house of God that held no message of joy within it.

And finally it was over.

Because it was expected he turned to face her and lifted the veil slowly. The church had been a place of refuge for him as a child and he still believed in the sanctity of religion despite everything he had become. The woman who stood there, however, was different from the laughing brave one in his bedchamber in Alderworth. This girl had dark rings beneath her lashes and eczema on her cheeks. Her eyes were flat blue orbs with no sparkle at all and the bump on her head from the accident was still visible. Exhaustion wove paleness into her skin.

As hurt as he was. A shared damage.

He felt his hand move to touch the wound and stopped himself. Theirs was a marriage in name only and the Wellinghams had been insistent that he understood this was for public consumption. A week or two at the most and then they wanted him gone. Her brothers had said that was her wish, too, his bride who, after uttering only lies, would not carry out even the pretence of a union once her ruin was minimised.

A travesty. A perversion. A shameful parody of something that should have been finer. Lord, the notion that survival justified the use of immoral means to achieve the required end was rubbing off on him in a melancholic and peculiar discontent. *'He who neglects what is done for what ought to be done effects his ruin...'* Machiavelli. The memory took him back to the night she had burst uninvited into his room, her colour high and the red dress low across her breasts.

Tay wished Lucinda Wellingham would take his hand again and hold it as she had at Alderworth, her fingers entwined into the worth of him as if she knew things that nobody else had ever discovered. He shook his head hard at such nonsense and she chose that moment to look at him directly, pale blue searingly condemnatory, the lies between them settling into an uncrossable distance.

'It cannot be easy to be the bride of ruin.' His words made her flinch, but he did not take them back. He wished that amongst those gathered there had been one person who might have welcomed his company. But there wasn't. All the wives of the Wellinghams had drawn Lucinda into their bosom, their eyes slicing across his like sharp knives—a rancorous truce, the white flag of surrender raised across his spilled blood and bruising. If he had by chance dropped dead due to some unforeseen and dreadful ailment he thought a party might have ensued, this veil of pretence transformed into a celebration of death.

He had never felt so unwelcome anywhere.

The shake of Taylen Ellesmere's head made Lucinda turn away, the tears she felt smarting at the back of her burning eyes threatening to fall. He did not look contrite or penitent or even slightly apologetic. He looked implacable and indifferent, this man who had disgraced her through fine red wine and a callous disregard for innocence, and was now making no effort whatsoever to assuage such poor behaviour.

The Bride of Ruin, indeed. Her husband now. Judas. Shylock. Marcus Brutus.

Lucinda could not even bear the thought that he might reach out and touch her.

She had been destroyed and she could remember none of it. She had been deflowered by a master with only the slightest jolt of memory remaining. Her brothers stood around her, a wall of masculine prickliness, sheltering her from the canker this betrothal had spawned, her sisters-in-law stalwart in the next ring of protection.

Alderworth had not apologised to them. Rather he had laughed in the face of their accusations and sworn free will was a liberty that all were entitled to.

Free will to take an innocent beneath him and to ravish her under the influence of strong wine; free will to take her to his bed and to say nothing to obliterate the raging gossip that swirled around the circles of society.

Lucinda Wellingham, the harlot. Lucinda Wellingham, intrinsically flawed.

Like the spoilt centre of a fruit, she thought, and was glad Posy Tompkins had also pushed in beside her because at least her friend's perception of the nuptials was laced with some sense of excitement.

'You will be free now, Luce. A married woman has so many more liberties.'

'I doubt another invitation will ever land upon my mantel, Posy.'

'Then we shall hold our own soirées, brilliant cultured gatherings that shall be the talk of the town.'

'Like courtesans?' Lucinda could not take the sting of it from her words for, all of a sudden, the whole world seemed meaningless and hollow. Posy had no notion of the signed agreements designating the boundaries of this marriage. She had not told her.

'Taylen Ellesmere is titled and handsome. There will be many a woman who might envy you such a husband. Believe me, be thankful he was not old and grey with no teeth and bad breath.'

Despite everything Lucinda smiled. Trust Posy to see the bright side of it all. Taking her friend's hand, she held her fingers in a tight grip and turned away from the worry of her family. The promises had been given and the deed was done. The only way on from here was upwards and Lucinda swore that when she was finally free of all this she would never allow her life to be mired again in such a shambolic wreck of betrayal.

'The wedding breakfast has been set up, Lucy. Asher asked if you would come now so that we can get this…finished with.' Beatrice spoke softly so that no one would overhear. The Wellinghams could manipulate to avoid disaster, but they wanted no others to understand that they did so. The twenty or so outside guests who had strong ties with the family beamed at her from one corner of the room of Falder House.

They had been invited to make this farce seem… legitimate. With the knowledge of what might happen next her brothers had at least given her back her shattered name. But after this she would only garner pity; the bride who was left summarily by a husband who had never loved her.

Threading through the room, Beatrice, Taris and

Asher led the assembly along to the blue salon. If she had wondered before at the control her brothers liked to wield, she understood now the very essence of it. The tables were dressed lavishly, the settings of the finest bone china and sterling silver. French wine had been brought up from the cellar. No shortcuts to encourage gossip. No small errors that might make the invited guests wonder. Nay, beneath the polite banter another reality lingered, stronger and unmistakable, but only if your name was Wellingham.

Taylen Ellesmere was sat next to her, his nearness making her shake, though when his leaf-green eyes brushed her own she felt…dizzy and disorientated.

Some worry leaked through her anger, a quiet emotion in a room full of tension. Bruising lay beneath his one blackened eye and there was a cut upon his bottom lip that she had not noticed before. Despite it all his beauty shone through, no slight comeliness, either, but a full-on barrage of masculine grace.

Unnerved, she shifted the lengthy veil which had pulled in beneath her, the lace of the Carisbrook's heirloom fragile in the play of sunshine from the window. She felt as though the breath had been knocked out of her lungs by one hefty punch of misgiving, but another truth also lingered.

Her husband was not all evil. There was a goodness in him that no one had discovered as yet.

She knew this as certainly as night followed the day, even though on his left hand beside his marriage band other rings glinted in the light—perhaps reminders of love from other women he had once admired before he had been made to marry her by her brothers? His name was always linked to paramours, after all. Was there one who he might have wished was standing here now in her stead?

Her cheeks itched with the eczema she always got when misgiving consumed her and the idea that her good name might be salvaged by such a course of action suddenly seemed foolish and ill advised. She wished she did not feel so shamefully heated by his presence at her side, the indifference she sought so far away from this undeniable awareness of him.

'The carriage accident hurt us both? I have been told how very lucky I was in not being killed by it, for with only a small movement things could have been so very much worse and I may never have walked again or even spoken and according to Doctor Cameron there might have—'

He stopped her by raising one hand. 'Are you nervous?'

For the first time she could ever remember in her whole entire life, Lucinda blushed. She felt the slow crawl of blood fusing her cheeks and held her hand up to the heat.

'Why would you say that?'

'Because you confided in me once that you talk too much when you worry.'

Her mouth dropped open.

Such a private honesty and one that she had never let another soul be privy to. She seldom shared her secrets, keeping them close to her heart instead, safe from derision or discussion. When and why had she told him such a thing? Perhaps the wine had made her speak? The exasperating fact of her lack of memory was both tiring and worrying.

'Surely you remember. It was just before I kissed you.'

Should she tell him that only a minuscule recollection remained from the time that they had shared in his chamber? *His nakedness. The wine. His mouth upon her breast. Her nipples hardening.*

Now that was new. Sitting up, she tried to remember some more, but couldn't. A new resolution firmed. He had taken her maidenhood without her consent and now would pay for it.

The laws of the land were there to protect the innocent and every Lord in his position had been brought up to acknowledge such a code. Ethics safeguarded chaos. When such tenets were broken, this was the result: a hasty marriage between strangers, flung together by the flimsy strands of expedience.

'I was foolish to come to your house in the first place, your Grace, and more foolish to stay. This is my penance.' She kept her tone distant, formal, just a polite conversation. When she leaned forwards she caught sight of herself in the wide shiny silver of an unused platter. Her cheeks were worse, even in the few short hours since leaving her chamber. She doubted she had ever looked quite so awful and her groom's handsome visage just made everything a hundred times more humiliating. Shallow, she knew, but in all her girlhood fantasies she had not imagined herself appearing so very bedraggled at her own wedding feast.

Lord Fergusson came up behind them, placing one hand on each of their shoulders. 'If you can have a marriage like I had for forty-three years, then you will be well blessed.' His old eyes brimmed with kindness.

Tay Ellesmere simply looked across at her. Answer this as you will, he seemed to be saying, shards of irritation noticeable.

'Indeed, Lord Fergusson,' she replied, remembering Mary-Rose, his beautiful wife, who had passed away suddenly the previous summer.

'But may I offer you a few words of advice? What you put into a marriage is what you get out from it and agreement is the oil that smoothes the way.'

'Then with all the agreements between us, ours shall run most smoothly,' Alderworth observed.

He had changed the meaning of the word 'agreement', but Lord Fergusson did not understand his reference. Her new husband's hands were in his lap. Fisted. Not quite as indifferent as he made out to be. Another thought struck her. Every knuckle had been grazed as though he had only recently been in a fight. Was that why his eye was black and his jaw cut? Please, God, let it not have been her brothers who had hurt him.

'I knew your uncle, Duke.' This was said tentatively. 'The Earl of Sutton.'

'Unfortunate for you.' Her groom's tone was plain ice and Lord Fergusson left as quickly as he had come, a frown on his face as he scrambled away.

'He is an old man who would do you no harm, your Grace, and he has only just lost his wife. Besides, this is a wedding and people expect—'

He broke in before she had finished. 'What do they expect, Lucinda? All that is between us here is dishonesty and farce. The charade of a marriage and the farce of a happy ever after. And now you want me to lie about an uncle who was not fit to be around children, let alone one who—' He stopped suddenly, his green eyes as dark as she had ever seen them, fathomless pools of torture. The real Taylen Ellesmere who lived beneath all he showed to the world was evident, the pain within him harrowing.

'You speak about yourself as a child? This uncle, the Earl of Sutton, he was your guardian?'

Only horror showed now, though the shutters reflecting emotion closed even as she watched and the implacable ruthless Duke was back.

'Enjoy your day, my dearest wife, because there are not many left to us.'

With that he stood and walked out of the room.

Chapter Five

God, she knew. Lucinda Alice Ellesmere was guessing his secrets as easily as if he had written them down for her, one after the other of sordid truth.

He should have remained silent, but the old man and his useless dreams had rattled him, made him remember his own hopes as his mother and father had spat and hissed each and every word to the other, unmindful of a small child who heard the endless malice and rancour. He had promised himself he would never marry and yet here he was, chained to a family who would like nothing better than to see him dead and buried.

'If you slope off now you won't get a penny, Alderworth.' Cristo Wellingham came to his side, the room they were in empty. Unexpectedly Lucinda's youngest brother produced a cheroot. 'You have the look of a man who might need one,' he said, offering a light and waiting as Tay took the first few puffs.

Smoke curled towards the ceiling, a screen of white and then gone. Tay wished he could have disappeared as easily as it did and, closing his eyes for a second, he leaned back against the wall, enjoying the first rush of its effects.

'I look forward to the day when the guilt of your sister's lies finally brings her to her senses.' The exhaustion in his voice was disconcerting, but the day had taken its toll and he was tired of the pretence.

'When you will likely be squandering what is left of your blood money in some poverty-stricken dive, remembering the ill that you did to a blameless innocent and wondering how you came to such a pass.'

He laughed at that. 'You did not enjoy a few of your wife's charms before marrying her?' A shadow rewarded the query and so he continued. 'I kissed your sister and brought her home. That was all. If she insists otherwise, then I say she lies.'

'With a reputation as disreputable as your own, a lack of belief in anything you say cannot be surprising.'

'Then allow me one boon, Lord Cristo. Allow me the small privilege of some knowledge of how your sister fares once I have gone.'

'Why would you want that? You have made it plain enough that a substantial payment constitutes the sum total of your care.' He stepped back. 'There won't be more from where that came from, no matter what you might say.'

'You will always hold her safe, then?' Tay had

not meant to ask the question, but it slipped from him like a living thing, important and urgent, the last promise he might extract before he was gone.

'Safer than you damn well did,' came the reply, but in Cristo Wellingham's dark eyes puzzlement flickered. Using it to his advantage, Taylen pressed on.

'If I wrote, would you give her my letters?'

'Yes.' Ground out, but honest. When Lucinda's brother turned and left he was glad he had been given even that slight hope of contact.

Lucinda felt exhausted by all the smiles and good wishes given with such genuine congeniality that the scandal disappeared into a God-ordained union that restored the balance of chaos in a highly regulated world. A violation covered up. A wrong righted. A happy ending to a less-than-salubrious beginning.

She had been surprised at the way the Duke of Alderworth had stood next to her for the past twenty minutes, his manner with the guests at odds with his self-proclaimed lack of interest in polite society. Perhaps he, too, had finally seen that in a good show of pretence there lay freedom. When his arm touched hers the full length of warmth seared in, the shock of contact electric, her breath held still by an awareness that she had felt with no other before him.

If only she might remember what a night in his bed felt like. The very idea made her frown, because in it she sensed she was missing something important.

'You look concerned.' Alderworth used a gap in the line of well-wishers to address her directly.

'It seems for all your reputation, people here are inclined to give you a second chance. I was wondering why.'

'Perhaps it's because you stand up as my bride, a Wellingham daughter who might deign to lend her name to my sullied one.'

'No. It is more than that. They accord you a certain begrudging respect, which is interesting.'

'Vigilance might be a more apt word!' Unexpectedly he smiled at her, the green in his eyes relaxing into gold, and with the colour of his skin burnished into bronze by the outdoors and his dark hair so shortened, he looked…unmatched. Her brothers were handsome, but the Duke had some spark of incomparable beauty that set him apart from everyone else Lucinda had ever seen.

The vapidity of her thoughts held her mute.

'Frowning does not suit you as much as laughter does,' he remarked.

'Of late there has not been too much to be delighted by.'

'I am sorry for that.'

'Are you?' Even amidst a crowd of family friends she could not leave the question unvoiced.

She saw him glance around to check the nearness of those in his vicinity before he gave a reply.

'I lived with lies all of my childhood, Duchess, and do not wish to encourage them. If you insist on such deception then that is your prerogative, but I will never understand it.'

Both her new title and his unwarranted anger made Lucinda step back, the same scene she had remembered at the breakfast table a week ago replaying over and over in her head.

His nakedness, the red wine, the feel of his warm skin against her own. The door locked and the key hidden. No opportunity to simply leave.

'London is a haven for gossip, Duke, and because of your actions my name has been slandered from one edge of it to the other.'

'A reputation lost for nothing, then.'

Lucinda paled. Did he speak of her virginity in such scathing terms? She was glad her brothers were nowhere nearby to hear such an accusation.

'For nothing?' She could barely voice the question. 'You are a reprobate, your Grace, of the highest order and the fate that flung us together at Alderworth will be regretted by me for the rest of my life. Bitterly.' There was no longer any conciliation in her tone.

He had the temerity to smile. 'Then it is a shame you did not make full use of our evening together and understand the true benefits that uninhibited sensuality can bring. Better to have enjoyed a night in my bed learning all you needed to know about the art of love and regretted it, than repenting the "nothing" you have been crucified for.'

Shocked, she turned on her heels and left him, not caring who saw her flee. He would castigate her for her poor performance in bed when she could recall none of it. Her blood rose to boiling and she hated her pronounced limp.

'Are you feeling well, Lucinda?' Emerald waylaid her before she had reached the door.

'Very.' Even to a beloved sister-in-law she couldn't betray him entirely, a trait she did not understand at all.

'Alderworth will be gone before the end of this week and you will never need to see him again.'

The absurdity of such a statement suddenly hit her, the first glimpse of her life after today. Was she destined then to always be alone, marriage-less and childless? Would she now linger in the corner of society with those hapless spinsters who spoke of unrequited love or of no love at all? Not ruined, but blighted by her lack of adherence to the normal conventions and suffering because of it.

The headache she had been cursed with all day bloomed with a fierce pain, blurring her vision. A migraine. She had had them badly ever since the accident.

Understanding her malady, Emerald took her hand and led her from the room, the familiar flight of stairs to her childhood bedroom welcomed. A refuge. A place to hide.

With care Emerald helped her undress and pulled down her hair till it fell about her waist, the heaviness of it causing her temples to throb harder.

'Marriage has made everything worse, Emmie.' The ring Alderworth had brought with him glinted on her finger and she looked down at it. A single ruby in white gold. Surprisingly tasteful. 'Before it was only my reputation immured in the sludge, now it is my whole life as well.'

'When your head does not ache as much and you realise you can once again participate in all the things you love doing, the world will look rosier.'

'As a widow? As a wife? As a spinster for ever doomed to sit in the corner, waiting for a husband who is gone?'

'You are saying that you wish he would not disappear?' Her sister-in-law's voice was sharp.

'No.' Shaking her head violently, she remembered Taylen Ellesmere's caustic disparagement of that which had been between them. She also remembered the way it had felt when their arms had touched and he had not pulled away.

She shook away the thought with a hard anger. Her husband saw her as a woman to be pitied, a poor excuse of a girl with her puritanical take on life and her inability to embrace his darkness.

They would ruin each other. It was as simple as that. All she wanted was to be between cool and crisp linen sheets, the world dissolved into dreams and ease and far from the reality of being bride to a groom who had not said even one kind word to her across the whole awful charade of their wedding day.

The Bride of Ruin. Indeed, she was exactly that.

'Lucinda is in bed with a headache and won't be joining the family again this evening. To say that she is disappointed in you would be putting it mildly.'

Asher Wellingham stood before Tay, a glass of brandy in a sizeable goblet in his hand. He did not offer the chance of the same to him. Taris Wellingham leant against a window in the far end of the library. As reinforcement, Taylen supposed, the quiet stillness of the middle brother as alarming as it always was.

'You will be allotted a chamber here, Alderworth, to allay any rumour or gossip. Then you will accompany Lucinda to the Parkinsons' ball tomorrow evening. The Duchess and I will attend as well, to make certain that you play the part of a doting and besmitten groom.'

'Another staged affair, then, though I cannot quite understand what you plan to do about the legal fact of our union in the future. Marriage is usually for ever.'

'Death negates a marriage.' The words were said without any emotion whatsoever as amber eyes met his own.

'You are threatening me?'

'I am the head of a family who is trying to make sense of a senseless act of treachery.'

'Treachery? I kissed your sister once and then

bundled her into the carriage to bring her home. An accident prevented us from reaching this town house. Where is the treachery in that?'

'I am more inclined to believe my sister's version of the story above your own.'

'The ravished, ruined version?' Tay could not help his sarcasm and the Duke of Carisbrook's brow furrowed.

'If I hear even the slightest hint of rumours that you say differently, I will make it known you demanded money from us for the sole purpose of your own benefit. Blackmail, if you will, with no thought for your innocent bride.'

'A fabrication that will have me drummed out of London whilst you condemn Lucinda to the life of a nun?'

'Better a nun than the harlot you have already made her.'

'Better than a misguided girl who invents tales to trap me?' Tay had had enough of carefully tip-toeing around the issue and the gloves were off.

Intent darkened his adversary's eyes. 'You came into our lives by an accident, Alderworth, and you can depart on one just as easily.'

'More threats?'

Turning away from Asher Wellingham, Taylen took in a breath. Let him strike like a coward and see what happened next. He had had it with headaches and warnings just as he had had it with utter lies. This was his wedding night and the only one he might damn well ever get, given these ridiculous edicts, yet here he was trading insults with his…new brother-in-law. Such a thought made him maudlin.

He could not win any concessions here tonight when tension, mistrust and fury coated every word between them. Better to wait until the morrow and have a conversation with his new bride that was long overdue.

'I am returning to my own town house and, short of rendering me unconscious and tying me up to a bed here, you can do nothing to stop me going. I will be back tomorrow after midday in the hope that your sister will be well enough to sit down and talk sense. Make sure that she is here, Carisbrook.'

As the door closed and Alderworth's footsteps receded into the distance, Taris rose. 'There is a note in his voice that concerns me, Ashe.'

'How so?'

'He seems to genuinely believe he is the innocent party.'

'The guilt of the damned is never simple. His is just more complicated than most.'

Taris drained his glass. 'Emerald said that Lucy never wants to see him again.'

'A difficult emotion, given that a marriage ceremony has just been performed and he was promised a week.'

'We might be rid of him if we were to leave London at first light and make for somewhere he could not find us. I think both parties need some time to take stock of what has happened and see a way through this. I doubt he would make a fuss with the threat of the removal of the promised remuneration hanging over his head.'

Possibilities roared between them as the fire carved shadows across the ceiling. A clean break would make certain that Lucinda was safe and it would also calm the troubled waters until they might make something else of the conundrum. The fine strong brandy in each of their glasses after such a harrowing day made their best intentions seem more…persuasive, less high-handed.

Always they had cared for their little sister, rescuing her from this scrape and then that one, smoothing down conjecture and controlling any whispered gossip. Always, until now.

'Have we made a mistake, do you think, insisting on this damn marriage?' Asher's voice was grave, copious liquor and contrasting emotions clouding certainty.

'Too late for second thoughts.' Taris swore even as he said it, a ripe curse that reverberated around the library. 'We did what we could. It is far past time for Lucy to understand the repercussions of her mistakes.'

'Loneliness might be one of them.'

'Aye, it might. But better than being tied to a man she loathes, I'd be thinking, and if we play it right he will be gone and she can get on with a new sort of life. These awkward alliances happen all the time, but with good management they can be manipulated to appear to be nothing like they actually are.'

'Successful?' Sarcasm dripped from the word.

'I was thinking more along the lines of moderately satisfactory to both parties concerned. Lucinda gets her freedom and Alderworth his money. At least it is a way past ruin.'

Chapter Six

Hands kept shaking her awake, insistent and un-relenting.

'Come, Lucy, we need to be up and about, for Asher wants us out of London by daybreak.'

'Why?'

Taking a quick look at the clock on her bedside table, Lucinda determined it to be very early in the morning. The birds had not even called yet and Emerald looked in a hurry.

'Alderworth is rescinding his promise to leave. He seems to think you will be accompanying him north to his estate.'

Sitting up, Lucinda pushed the covers back, the bruises on her legs dark against the whiteness of the sheets.

'He wants that of me?'

Her sister-in-law shrugged her shoulders. 'Given his character he probably wishes to haul you off to Alderworth and keep you there.'

'Like a prisoner?' Tremors of fear made her feel ill.

'Of course not. But it might behove us to make certain that he understands exactly what you do want.'

'Nothing. I wish for nothing between us.'

The wedding dress stared at her from its hanger across the wardrobe door, the white, pristine silk more than she could bear. Getting up, she threw the thing into the cupboard, the veil of gauzy lace joining it.

One day when she was ninety and her brother's children's children asked her about her life, she might tell them that the worst moment of all was the one where she had caught sight of herself in the mirror in her bedroom the morning after her nuptials. And when they asked her why, she would say because that was the moment she realised there would never be another chance of happiness for her.

'I will have the housekeeper dispose of the gown, Lucinda, so that you do not need to see the garment again.' Emerald's eyes were a stormy turquoise, but tenderness lay in the hand that came to fall over hers. 'We shall get through this together as a family, for your brothers have ways to right all the wrongs.'

'Divorce is not an easy passage…'

'Annulment, then? That could be an option.'

'I rather think that might have come too late, considering my returning memories and society's talk. I should never have married him at all.'

'Then we just need some time to think about it,

some quiet time away from the pressures of London. A solution is always available to any problem and this one will be no different.'

'What if Alderworth comes to find me at Falder and demands my return?'

The silence told her that there was some other thing afoot.

'We are not going to Falder?'

'No. We are making for Beaconsfield and then to a house on the south coast. You can live there with a stipend if you cannot stay close to town.'

'Away from the Duke of Alderworth?'

'He is a dangerous adversary, Lucy. Until we can formulate a plan to keep you safe, it is better to keep you apart. I think such a man would insist on his marital rights.'

The blood simply drained from her face as she contemplated that truth. Would the Dissolute Duke want to take her to his bed? Again? Her imagination ran wild. If she was already pregnant from her ignominious ruin, how would this change things? The very thought of it had her reaching for her thick night-wrap.

'I do not want to see him, Emmie. Asher is right. I wish for some distance between us so that I can indeed think.'

Tay sat in his study with the curtains open and a quarter-moon outside in the heavens struggling to find clear sky through banks of high-billowed cloud.

She had left. Lucinda Wellingham had gone with her family from London, running in the early dawn to a place that was not Falder. He had found out this little information from a stable hand he waylaid on the way home from their town house, though the boy had no inkling of their true destination.

His bride had, however, left a note, the words written in his memory like some morbid poem of rebuttal.

I hope that you will allow me a few weeks to recover from the accident and to consider my options.

Please do not come after me. I will not receive you.

If you need to contact me, Cristo will forward any communication and I will answer as I see fit.

The missive was signed formally. *Lady Lucinda Wellingham.* She had not even used his name.

Lifting a glass of brandy to his lips, he upended it, the quiet tonight a pressing and heavy one. The purse of the Wellinghams sat on the desk in front of him, a considerable sum representing a new life, somewhere far from England, perhaps? The Americas beckoned and so did the East Indies. Here he was struggling to keep ahead of the many and mounting debts his father had left him, every pound he made subtracted twice over by the ones he owed. Another few years at this rate and it would all be gone. Alderworth, the extensive land and buildings around it and the London town house, disappeared into the gloom of history.

A new life summoned—a refurbishment of the soul and one with a beguiling promise. The choice was simple. Stay here and fight the power of the Wellinghams for a wife who did not want him, or leave on a new tide and chance his hand at something different. He had never travelled away from the shores of England before, the duties of being the caretaker of Alderworth taking all his attention. If he left half of the Wellingham money here in an account to be drip-fed into the estate just to keep it afloat, perhaps he could build other possibilities?

Flat blue eyes came to mind, the anger in them directed only at him. Lucinda wanted neither his name nor his title and, as tiredness settled, it took too much will to quarrel.

His parents had frittered away their lives together in acrimonious exchanges and he did not wish to do the same. No, far better to welcome change and simply vanish.

His eyes strayed to the band on the third finger of his left hand. To have and to hold from this day forth, his wife had promised as she had placed it there…

Dragging the gold across his knuckles, he threw it into a drawer in the desk. A relationship that had begun in untruth and blossomed under duress was now ended in deceit. He would journey to a far-off corner of the world which laid no claim to the stifling conventions of a society immured in manners.

And then he would be free.

The journey south was hurried and long and as the carriage swayed against a wind from the sea, Lucinda thought that her life from now on might be exactly like this flight into obscurity.

She could not go back and she could not go forwards, the worry of seeing Taylen Ellesmere again precluding any early return to London. Emerald and Asher both looked as tired as she did, the last weeks resting on their faces, worn down by worry. At least the beginning of her menses had come that morning and there was some relief to know she would not be bound to Alderworth by a child. But even that relief was tempered by sadness as she faced the possibility that she might never ever be a mother.

'The air here is so much better than in London, Ashe.' Emerald's observation was falsely cheerful, just words to fill in the heavy silence.

Lucinda nodded and tried to smile, though she doubted that her brother would be fooled by such a forced joviality. With a cursory glance at the sky, Asher brought the subject back to the problem they were all thinking about.

'In a month you can come back to Falder, Lucinda. I will employ guards to make certain Alderworth comes nowhere near you and at least it will be a more familiar setting. I doubt, however, that London will be a destination available to you for a good long while yet. Society has a great need to feed off scandal and this one...' He left the sentence unfinished.

She nodded to please him, but the ache in her breast threatened to explode into an anger she did not recognise. She wished with all her heart that she had not been persuaded to go to a house of such ill repute in the first place, for all that had followed was the result of one injudicious decision.

'Visiting Alderworth was more than foolish,' she muttered and Asher looked up, the pity in his eyes almost her undoing.

'I have left word to have Alderworth followed so any movements that alarm us will be monitored. Let us hope he has the sense to retire to that estate of his and never again leave it.'

'You think he will stay in England?' As Emerald asked the question something passed between Asher and her—a warning, were Lucinda to name it. A quiet notice of caution with an undercurrent of intent.

Goodness, had her brothers shanghaied her husband already and thrown him on to a ship sailing far from Britain before disgorging him on to some unknown foreign shore? Her mind ran all the possible injuries that Taylen Ellesmere might sustain.

'If you have hurt him...' she began and stopped, dread making her question what it was she was going to say. Ellesmere should mean nothing to her. She should be glad that he would disappear for ever, yet concern lingered.

'He is at liberty to go where he wants. There was no duress in it.'

'You paid him?' Suddenly she understood. 'You bribed him to leave?'

When he nodded, she looked away. Ruined and humiliated. She vowed that there would never be another time when she allowed a man to hurt her.

Tay watched the coast of England receding into only mist. The sea birds called around him as the canvas of the sails caught the wind, turning the ship east, and an excitement he had not felt before quickened his breath and made him lift his face to the heavens.

Free.

For the first time in his life the debt of Alderworth did not weigh him down with its constant demands and a new horizon beckoned.

A place to make a different mark, a land where no one knew him. The mantle of the past slipped away into the gathering breeze and his fingers curled around the guard rail, holding on to the rusted steel as though his very life depended on it.

'You look as though you could do with a drink.' A tall red-haired man stood next to him, the collar of his coat raised against the weather. 'Where are you headed?'

'Anywhere a fortune is to be made,' Tay answered, a plan formulating as he spoke. He needed money to come back. He needed good hard cash to retrieve his life and make it work in the way he wanted it to. His glance took in the bare third finger on his left hand as the stranger spoke again.

'I am bound for North Georgia. They say that the gold there is easy to retrieve and the veins are rich. Two years I have given myself to find it and my wife, Elizabeth, is already counting down the days.'

'You have experience of mining, then?' A small worm of an idea began to creep up into possibility.

The other nodded. 'With farming as it is I have needed to supplement my income from the family estate by other means. I could do with a partner if you are interested. A flat fee for the tools we will need and that will be it, save for lots of hard work and a good dollop of persistence. A sense of humour might help, too.'

The screech of a gull above had them looking up, the big bird wheeling out of the sky towards them, its wings outstretched as it landed on a point at the top of the ship. Hitching a ride or having a rest?

Choices.

They came from the most unexpected places and from the most unexpected people. Putting out his hand, he felt the firm grasp of the other.

'Tay Ellesmere.' No title. Nothing to tie him to the England he was leaving. A different man with another life.

'Lance Montcrieff. From Ridings Hall in Devon.'

Lucinda walked along the cliffs of Foulness Point and watched the ocean waves break across the beaches below, never-ending tides, washing the land clean of all that it had left there the day before. A constantly refreshed canvas, the flotsam of life taken away to another headland in a different place, redefined and transformed.

As she was not. Two years of isolated country living had left her struggling with her identity, Falder and its environs beautiful, but never changing. Her physical strength had returned finally, though her memory had never followed. Oh, granted, she still had headaches sometimes and when she was tired her vision became a little blurred, but the bone-wearying fatigue had dissipated and in its place a haunting curiosity had risen.

She wondered where in the world the Duke of Alderworth might now be. Cristo had given her a letter a good year ago and she had opened it with shaking fingers.

His description of a town in the North Georgia mountains in the Americas had been interesting, but had left her hollow. He had written nothing of his feelings or of his intentions or of any new relationships he might have formed. A half-page long, and wholly factual, the message could have been written for anyone.

He had signed it Tay Ellesmere. No title. Just the diminutive of Taylen. *Tay.* She had run the word a thousand times off her tongue ever since reading it and hated herself for doing so.

She wanted him back. She did, out here in the

wind and with the sound of the ocean all around her. She wanted to feel his skin against her own in that particular way he had of heightening her senses and making her feel alive.

Dead. She had been dead since he had left, on an early morning ship out of St Katherine's Dock, Asher had said. Sailing for the Americas and a new life without any of the burdensome encumbrances that he had been tied to in England and so unwillingly.

Paid to take ship from London and never return? She had heard that, too, when she had listened in to a conversation between Taris and Asher. All she had picked up in their tones was relief that Alderworth was gone and so she had tried to forget him, banishing all thoughts of a husband from her mind.

And failing.

She hated this limbo she was in, caught between marriage and widowhood, and never a chance of moving on. Sometimes she hated Taylen Ellesmere so much that her skin shook with the loathing.

A voice calling took her thoughts away and she saw Lord Edmund Coleridge, a friend of Cristo's, walking towards her.

'Cris told me that you would be here,' he said as he came close. 'He also said that I was to ask you for a dance tonight at Graveson.'

'Florencia's party?' The house had been awash with busy hands since it had been decided to throw a birthday party for Cristo and Eleanor's oldest daughter.

'Seven is an important number. She has asked her father if she might invite Bram Crowley to help her celebrate.'

'Young love.' Lucinda smiled and shook her head. Brampton's father owned the property bordering Cristo and Asher's holdings and, although the family were not titled, they were by all accounts very rich. Florencia had liked him from the very first moment she had arrived with her mother, and the boy had done much to bring a frightened and retiring child out of her shell.

'I hope you might save a waltz for me, Lady Lucinda.' Edmund took her hand, surprising her. 'I would dearly like to get to know you better.'

'I am married, my lord,' she returned quickly. 'There can be no gain in aiming your sights at me.'

His laughter floated on the wind around them, a happy, free sound that made her relax.

'Your brother told me that you were forthright and now I believe him. I will swap you one waltz for the chance to tool my greys around the Falder course on the morrow.'

'A difficult thing to refuse. Did Cris also tell you of my passion for horses?'

'He did indeed. He said I was to expound on my expertise in archery as well.' His eyes lost their humour as he continued. 'It is just a dance I beseech, Lady Lucinda, and the chance of friendship.'

For the first time in a long while Lucinda allowed a man to hold her fingers for more than a second without pulling away. There was none of the magic there that she had felt with Alderworth, but it was not unpleasant, either. With blond hair blowing in the wind and his dark eyes soulful, Edmund Coleridge had his own sort of appeal. Lord knew she had heard he was popular with all the young ladies of society and she could see how that could be so.

But he did not smell of wood-smoke and lemon and his eyes were not the colour of the wet forests at Falder. Nor were they underlaid with a thrilling lust that made her whole body sing.

Lucinda wore a new gown that evening, a red silk that was edged in gold. Such a combination might have been showy, but the dressmaker had played up the under-lights in the silk and matched them exactly with the trim.

'You look beautiful tonight, Lucy.' Emerald was the first to see her as she came downstairs, and indeed as she caught a reflection in the large mirror at Graveson she did look…different.

Sorrow had stalked her for so long since the fiasco in London that Lucinda had almost got used to its sombre presence. Tonight, however, her spirit was lifted. Perhaps it was because of something as uncomplicated as the beautiful gown or the fact that Eleanor's maid had fashioned her hair in a new style. Or perhaps it was just the fact of a family celebration and the excitement of Florencia, Cristo and Eleanor.

Edmund Coleridge was the next one to compliment her and he did so with a raft of words.

'I could compare your hair to moonbeams or sunlight or to the sparkling fall of water over rocks, my lady.'

Despite the flowery rhetoric, Lucinda laughed. 'Please do not, my lord.'

She liked the warmth of his hand and the smooth feel of his skin. His hair tonight was Macassared and it suited him; made him look more dangerous. She shook away the thought. Safety was what she was after. The consequences of following reckless paths had ruined everything, after all, and she had promised herself to walk a discreet and scatheless way in future.

'Your niece has been asking after you. I think she wants to give you something.'

As if on cue Florencia appeared before them, a beautiful gardenia in hand. 'Everyone has to wear one tonight, Aunty Lucy, because they are my very favourite flower.'

Lucinda noticed the bottom of the stalk had been wrapped in brown paper, a pin secured in the folds.

'Is this your handiwork, my love?' she asked as she took the bloom and smelt it.

'Mine and Mama's.' Her dark eyes crossed to Edmund. 'But you are wearing yours upside down.' A wide smile lit up her face as Coleridge knelt and fashioned his flower exactly as she wanted it.

'Is this better?'

'Much. Now I just have to find Uncle Taris. I think he is hiding from me because he thinks flowers are for girls.'

With a whirl she was gone, with her little basket of gifts and a jaunty lilt to her step. Lucinda remembered back to when she had first met Cristo's daughter. The change in her demeanour was heartening and it seemed Coleridge was thinking exactly the same thing.

'Cris is lucky with his family and is happier than I have ever seen him.' The flower had wet the fabric of his coat where water seeped through the paper, but he only wiped it away.

Edmund Coleridge was a kind man, a good man with high principles and moral worthiness. She caught Eleanor watching them with a smile on her face and thought briefly how easy it might have been had she chosen a man like this one. Her family liked him, society lauded his goodness and he observed her as though he was inclined to know her better.

When a waiter passed with a tray of drinks in tall and fluted glasses she picked one up and drank it quickly before returning for a second.

'My brother knows his wine. French, I should imagine, and very smooth.'

The first flutter of warmth stirred in her stomach, the drink relaxing a tension that was ever-present in her life. More usually she stayed away from anything that might not allow her control, after her last débâcle, but tonight she felt able to risk it.

She nodded as Edmund Coleridge took her hand and asked her to dance. A waltz, she realised, as he led her to the floor, the slow languid three-beat music swirling across her senses.

He was thinner than his clothes suggested, but as her fingers came across the superfine of his jacket a sense of masculine strength made her breath come faster. It had been so long since she had touched a man like this.

Taylen.

Swallowing, she made herself stop. Alderworth was not here and would never be so. He had gladly gone to the Americas, paid handsomely by her brothers to abandon any husbandly duty. The ache in her chest made her breathe faster.

'We can sit this out if you would wish to?'

Concerned dark eyes washed across her own.

'No. I would like to dance.'

The music of the orchestra was beautiful and the smell of the gardenia wafted up from her gown. She had to learn to live again, to laugh and to dance and to touch a man without pulling back. The wine was beginning to weave its magic and at the side of the room she could see Asher and Emerald watching her without worry marking their eyes.

Two years of dislocation. The silk of her chemise felt cool against her skin and Edmund Coleridge's fingers curled with an increasing pressure around her own.

Claimed. Quietly. She did not look up at his face.

Too soon. Too quick. She wished the fingers that held her own were covered in golden rings, an old scar visible just beneath the crisp white cuff of shirt.

Taylen.

Sometimes she could smell him, at night when everything was still and when she reached into the deepest place of memory. Lemon, woodsmoke and desire. She bit at her bottom lip and sent the thought scattering, leaf-green laughing eyes and short dark hair dissolving into nothingness.

'Will you come back to London soon?'

Another voice. Higher.

Edmund.

'I am not entirely certain. My brothers think that I should, but...'

'Come with me, then. Let me take you to the Simpson Ball.'

Now his interest was stated and affirmed, the *perhaps* that Lucinda had been enjoying transformed into certainty. The game of courtship had begun, all chase and hunt, and her heart sank.

'I am a married woman, my lord.'

'A married woman without a husband.' The dimples in his cheek made him look younger than he was, an amiable and gracious man who had taken the time and effort to try to humour a woman of little joy. Cristo's friend, and a man that her other brothers approved of, all the parts of him adding up to a decent and honest whole.

She allowed him the small favour of bringing her

closer into the dance so that now his breath touched her face.

'I should like to see you laugh, Lucinda.' When his thighs pushed against her own, the pulse in his throat quickened. Coleridge was so much easier to read than Alderworth had ever been, his secrets hidden in an ever-present hardened core of distrust.

Breaking off the dance when the music finished, Edmund led her into the conservatory at the head of the room. Stars twinkled through the glass overhead and myriad leafy plants stood around them in the half-light.

She knew he would kiss her even before he leaned down, she could see it in his eyes and on his face, that desire that marks even the most timid of men. She did not push him away, either, but waited, as his lips touched her own, seeking what it was all lovers sought, the magic and the fantasy.

A light pressure and then a deeper one, his tongue in her mouth, finding and hoping. She felt his need and tried not to stiffen, understanding his prowess, but having no desire for a mutual understanding. Just flesh against flesh, the scrape of his teeth upon her lip, his wetness and the warmth. Ten seconds she counted and then twenty until he broke away, a flush in his cheeks and a hoarseness of breath.

Sadness swamped her as he brought her in against him. Nothing. An empty nothingness. Wiping away the taste of him when he was not looking, the weft of cotton felt hard against her mouth.

'Thank you.' His words. Honourable and kind.

Even as she tried to smile an aching loss formed, the mirthless harbinger of all that she had wasted. Alderworth had ruined her in more ways than he knew. Edmund Coleridge was exactly the sort of beau she should wish to attract and yet…

'Perhaps we should go inside. It is chilly out here.' The shaking she had suddenly been consumed by was timely.

'Of course, my dear. A dress of silk is no match even for a summer evening. I should have realised.'

Manners and courtesy. The smile on her face made the muscles in her cheek ache as she accompanied him into supper.

'Edmund seems more than taken with you, Lucy.' Cristo approached her as she returned from having a word with Beatrice. 'He is a good man who has long wished to know you better.'

'Well, I am sure he is besieged by all the lovely young women in society. His manners are faultless and he is such congenial and unaffected company.'

Cristo frowned. 'Such vacuous praise is usually an ominous sign…' His dark eyes watched her, the gold in them easily seen in the light from the chandeliers above.

Lucinda rapped him with her fan. 'I am not in the market for a…dalliance.'

He laughed at that, tipping his head up with mirth, the sound booming around them.

'I hope not. It was something more permanent Edmund was angling for, I would imagine.'

Taking one of her hands, he chanced offering advice. 'If you do not choose to move on with your life soon, Lucy, the opportunities may not keep coming.'

'You speak of suitors as if I were a widow, Cris.' Anger tinged her words and she was surprised as he shepherded her from the salon and down the corridor to his library. Once there he poured himself a generous brandy, restoppering the decanter when she turned down the chance of the same.

'Another letter has come.'

The words shocked her. She felt the blood drain from her cheeks and her heartbeat race.

'From Alderworth? When?'

'Last week. The mark on it is from Georgia.'

'Yet you did not think to give it to me sooner?'

'I knew Edmund would come tonight and he had asked me for the chance to court you. I had hoped…'

'Hoped for what? Hoped that the law might have dissolved all that was between me and Alderworth? Hoped that I might finally find a man that you all approved of? Hoped that the scandal of my disgrace may have been watered down by the pure goodness of your friend? That sort of hope?' Her voice had risen as she shook away his excuse. 'Where is it?'

Digging into a drawer at the back of his desk, Cristo laid an envelope down on the table. The writing was large and bold and not that of her husband, for the hand was completely different from the one correspondence she had received. Her excitement faded.

Lady Lucinda Ellesmere.

Graveson.

Essex.

Lucinda held her fingers laced together so they would not snatch at the paper. Was Taylen dead? Was this a missive to tell her of an accident or an illness or of the wearying of soul and a final resting place?

Had he married again, had children to a new lover, found gold, lost a hand, suffered a horrible and gruelling death in the throes of dysentery or smallpox or the influenza?

Finally she moved forwards and picked it up. 'Have you told Ashe of this?'

He shook his head.

'Then please do not.'

'You need to be careful, Lucy. Alderworth is a reprobate and a liar. He uses women for his own means and does not look back over his shoulder at whom he has hurt. Coleridge, on the other hand, is trustworthy.'

The sound of the orchestra winding up an air and the deep voice of Asher took them from the moment.

'The speeches.' Lucinda was glad for the interruption.

'We need to return to the ballroom.'

Folding the note, she stuffed it into a small compartment on one side of her reticule. Cristo made no comment as he gestured her to go before him and doused the lamp on his desk.

As soon as she was able to escape the party without raising any eyebrows Lucinda did so, climbing the steps to the room she had been allotted at Graveson with a mixture of hope and trepidation.

She could feel the presence of the envelope in her bag almost as a physical thing, prickling inwards.

Gaining her bedroom, she asked her maid to unhook the buttons at the back of her gown and, feigning tiredness, dismissed her. Locking the door behind the departing woman, Lucinda sighed with relief as she leaned back against heavy oak, free at last to see just what the letter from Georgia contained.

With agitation she slit open the top of the paper, carefully and precisely so as to do no damage to anything within.

A newspaper clipping confronted her, the folds of print displayed in such a way as to show a headline.

'Ellesmere strikes gold in fine style'.

The hazy distorted ink spoke of Tay Ellesmere celebrating with a great number of women in some sleazy saloon, the text citing details of a raucous party lasting well into the early hours of the morning, the guests invited unsuitable and rowdy.

As infamous as his soirées at Alderworth? Unchanged. Unabashed. She was in England pining for something that he had not spared a thought for, while he partied with women who were probably inclined to give away any and every favour he would want.

Swallowing, Lucinda let herself slide down the door frame where she sat pooled in red silk, her first finger tracing the exploits of a husband who on each turn of events seemed destined to disappoint her.

Another smaller piece of paper suddenly caught her eye and she lifted it up.

Lucinda

I presume that this is your runaway husband. Perhaps, given the goodly amount of his newly found claim, you should be seeking him out again.

I have sent this letter to Graveson in the hope that your brother might pass it on as I have no notion of your new address.

Yours

Anthony Browne

Screwing up the paper, Lucinda crossed the room to the fire, hurling the letter into the flames. The paper caught at one edge and blackened, embers glowing red before turning to a dull and dusty ash.

Anthony Browne, the brother of a school friend. She had always detested him.

Her glance returned to the newspaper cutting. If she had any sense she would consign this to the fire, too. But she didn't. She hated the tears that fell down her cheeks and the gulps of grief that she tried to quieten.

He would never stop hurting her, Taylen Ellesmere with his wild and ill-considered chaos. Another episode in a far-off land, his name slandered and his intentions dubious.

This was the man she had married, unstable, volatile and lawless.

Wiping the moisture away as a tear slid unbidden down the newsprint, she cradled the missive in her palm before bringing it to her heart.

'Where are you?' she whispered into the night.

Chapter Seven

London—1834

The gold coins were heavy in Tay's hand as he hoisted them up on to the desk. They clinked against the dark mahogany, solid and weighty, the letters of the Federal Mint at Atlanta imbued in red ink on the fabric of the bag.

'Here's the return of your bribe, Carisbrook, with more than interest in full. Now I want my wife back.'

Asher Wellingham stood as the words echoed around his library. 'You accepted our sum to disappear for ever.'

'Your expectation, Carisbrook, not mine. My Duchess and I shall leave for my country estate first thing in the morning and you can do nothing to stop us.'

'Over my dead body, you bastard.' Without warning the Duke was at Tay's throat before he had time to react, the chair beside the desk overturned and the strength of his fingers cutting off breath.

But Taylen was a good ten years younger than Lucinda's oldest brother and had more in muscle. His time in Georgia had also given him plenty of battle practice. With a quick twist he rolled away, fists up and waiting as the other angled in.

'I don't want to hurt you, Carisbrook. All I want is what is mine.'

'My sister isn't yours.'

'In God's eyes and anyone else that counts, Lucinda is my wife.' He had not meant to get into an argument, but the history between them was murky and here, in this same room he had been pummelled over once before, he found it difficult to temper back wrath.

'We should have killed you when we had the chance.'

Tay laughed and then moved quickly as a punch almost connected. He couldn't afford for his dinner dress to be bloodied as his next pressing destination was a ball. Waiting for his chance, he moved in, fingers reaching for the arteries of his adversary's throat.

It was over in two minutes, the point of pressure allowing an easy end. The fights in Dahlonega in Lumpkin County had been rough and a lucrative stake in gold at Ward's Creek in the North Georgia mountains always had to be defended. He almost felt sorry for the Duke of Carisbrook laid out on the floor but, when he checked, his breathing was deep and regular and tomorrow he'd barely feel any effects. Save embarrassment, probably, but he'd given Tay a good measure of the same treatment almost three years ago so Tay could not be remorseful.

Straightening his jacket, he caught sight of the clock at the end of the room. Ten-thirty. His wife was spending the evening at the Croxleys' ball in Culross Street and it wasn't far. He smiled. Almost too easy.

Letting himself out of the library, he closed the door behind him. Then he took his hat and cloak from the waiting servant and thanked him with a coin before walking into the night.

He was back.

She knew he was from the frantic whispers swirling around the ballroom, his name on the edge of every one of them.

'The Duke of Alderworth is here, returned from the Americas and twenty times richer than his father ever was.'

Lucinda felt all the eyes upon her as she stood near a pillar in the Croxleys' ballroom, Posy Tompkins to one side gripping her hand. Three years of dreading this very moment and it had finally arrived. The breath congealed in her throat and her heart beat so fast she was certain she would keel over.

No. She would not faint or fall or run. None of this was her fault, after all, and she would not allow Taylen Ellesmere to make her feel that it was.

'He is coming this way, Luce.' Posy barely managed to get the words out. 'And he is looking straight at us.'

'Then we shall give him exactly what he does not expect,' she replied, plastering a practised smile upon her face. Almost simple to do, she thought in surprise, the warmth of greeting a foil to the inquisitive faces turned her way.

'Your Grace.' Lucinda tried to make her tone convivial, a meeting of acquaintances, a trifling and inconsequential thing—a figure from the past to whom she had given no consideration since last seeing him.

'Duchess.' His voice had deepened in the years between their forced marriage and this unexpected return. 'I did not think to find you here in town.'

He was still beautiful. His hair was much longer than when she had seen him last and it made him look even more menacing.

Intimidating.

It was the only word she could come up with to describe him as he stood before her, dressed in black from head to foot, save for the white cravat at his neck fastened loosely in the style of a man without much care for fashion.

'Do you still enjoy the art of untruthfulness?'

The effrontery of such a question almost undid her and she answered with one of her own. 'Do you still enjoy despoiling innocents on a whim and all in the name of free will?'

A fiery glint in his eyes was seen fleetingly in a face hewn from cold stone.

Urbane and distant. Anger made her fists ball at her side, though she unclenched her fingers as soon as she realised what she was doing. She was pleased Posy had had the sense to retreat so that their conversation remained private.

'I had heard that you were back in England, your Grace.'

'Your brothers gave you the news, no doubt,' he returned, taking her hand in his own and pulling her towards the dance floor. 'But come, let's confuse the wagging tongues and stand up together. It will give us some space to talk.'

Short of creating a scene, Lucinda allowed herself to be led into a waltz, his arm encircling her back and drawing her towards him.

'The gossips have placed you on the Eastern seaboard coast of the Americas for many years, your Grace, taking part in all the temptations the cities there have to offer, no doubt.'

He laughed, a deep rumble of amusement; a man embedded in scandal and savouring it. Her ire rose unbidden. She had seen the evidence of his immorality, after all, in the headlined cutting Anthony Browne had sent her.

'Your brother Asher said much the same to me when I saw him this evening.'

'You have been to the Wellingham town house already? Why?'

'Paying my dues,' he replied obliquely, 'and stating my intentions.' He stopped for a moment as though gathering the gist of what he might next tell her. 'Not every one of them, though. I saved the best proposal of all for your ears only.'

A streak of cold dread snaked downwards. 'You want a divorce, no doubt?'

At that he laughed, the sound engulfing her.

'Not a divorce, my lady wife, but an heir, and as you are the only woman who can legitimately give me one the duty is all yours.'

She almost tripped at his words and he held her closer, waiting until balance was regained. Their eyes locked together, no humour at all in the green depths of Taylen Ellesmere, the sixth Duke of Alderworth.

He was deadly serious.

Shock gave her the courage of reply. 'Then you have a problem indeed, your Grace, because I am the last woman in the world who would ever willingly grace your bed again. Surely you understand why.' Disappointment and anger vibrated in her retort as strains of Strauss soared around them, the chandeliers throwing a soft pallor across colourful dresses resplendent in the room. The privilege of the *ton* so easily on show.

Scandal had its own face, too!

It came in the way his fingers held her to the dance even as she tried to pull away, and in the quiet caress of his skin over hers.

Memory shattered sense and the salon dimmed

into nothingness; the feel of his hands upon her nakedness, the smell of brandy and deceit and a wedding quick and harrowing in that small chapel.

Even the minister had not met her eye as he said the words, 'To have and to hold from this day forward…'

Taylen Ellesmere had stayed less than a few hours.

Her husband. A different and harder man from the one who had left her and now back for a legitimate heir. She wanted to slap him across his cheek in the middle of the ballroom and he knew it. It took all of her will not to.

'If there wasn't a male left in Christendom save for you, I still would not—'

He broke over her anger.

'I will gift you the sole use of the Alderworth London town house on the birth of our first son and pay you a stipend that will keep you independently wealthy in fine style.'

Blackmail and bribery now. She shook her head against such a promise, but did not speak.

'One heir and then the freedom to do whatever you want for the rest of your life. A safe haven. The power of independence and autonomy. One heir whom you shall have the right as a mother to raise until he is ten. Eton should see to the rest.'

'And if the child is a girl?'

'Then I will dissolve all contracts and allow you what I offer regardless. I would not tie you to such a bargain for ever should you in good faith produce only a female Ellesmere.'

She frowned, barely believing the words she was hearing. 'There are other women here who would jump at your offer, your Grace, if you obtained a divorce and remarried.'

'I know.'

'Then why?'

'Salvation.' He gave no other explanation as he smiled at her, the deep dimple in his right cheek caught in the light. So very beautiful.

Lucinda felt the muscles inside her clench.

Freedom for the use of her body? He had had his fill once and she was no longer young. The very memory of it all took her breath away.

'I will not rape you if that is what you are thinking.'

'A mutual consent may never happen, your Grace.' She put as much disdain into the words as she could manage.

'I stake all my gold on the fact that it will.' His voice was overlaid with a certainty that was worrying.

Could she do it? Play the whore to a husband she could not trust and sell her body for a freedom she had never had? The girl she had been almost three years ago now would never have considered such a monstrous proposition, but the woman she had become did.

'I want it in writing. I want a hundred pounds for

every time I lie with you and a hundred more for every month it takes to become pregnant. No one must know of this bargain of ours, however, and in public you will only sing my praises. Do you understand? I shall not be the subject of any scorn whatsoever, for if my brothers ever found out exactly what you have proposed…' She could not continue.

'They would offer more threats.' He said this not as a question but as a truth. 'However, I would like to add one more condition of my own. For the conception of an heir I would require the whole night in my bed, at a time of your choosing. No rushed affair. I wish to lie in the moonlight and know your body as well as you know it yourself. Hedonistic and unhurried.'

She turned her face away so that he would not see what she imagined might be there—horror vying with avidity. The muscles deep inside throbbed in a promise that was like the echo of memory. She would not show him the hurt or the anger or the plain recognition of the choking shame she had lived with since he had gone.

She would tell him none of it until she could take the papers for the town house and fashion a separate existence.

Salvation, he had said. Perhaps it would be hers as well, this unexpected departure from being beholden to her brothers' generosity and benevolence. The gossip that had never died down as she thought it would, but had followed her with every step that she took.

The forgotten wife. The abandoned bride. The willful Wellingham sister whose reckless antics had finally caught up with her.

'My carriage will collect you the day after tomorrow from Wellingham House and bring you up to my seat. It would be an early departure so you would need to make sure that you are ready when it arrives.'

She shook her head, sense returning in the indifferent way he gave her instruction, like a Lord might order his valet to set out his clothes. 'My brothers will stop me.'

'Then it is up to you to persuade them otherwise. But know that we are married in the face of God for ever. I have given you my terms of agreement and I would never consent to a divorce.'

When the music stopped he escorted her back to her place near the pillar and into the company of Posy.

'I shall expect you to be ready by nine o'clock on Thursday with any luggage you require. I will join you later on the Northern Road.'

Without further word, he left.

He had done it. He had struck the bargain that he needed with less difficulty than he might have imagined. The line of the Ellesmeres of Alderworth would be saved.

Tay breathed in hard even as he walked through the crowd, wondering why it was he felt so damned uncertain. His wife still wore the ring he had given her, he noticed. The rest of her fingers were bare. The scar on the back of her hand was faded now, but under the light from the chandeliers he had still been able to see it. The carriage accident had left marks inside and out. Shaking his head, he cursed.

She was a hundred times more beautiful than she had once been. He remembered her eyes to be darker, but they were the blue of the early spring-time sky, bright with promise. Her curves had matured as well, and her skin was still silky smooth and pale. He brought the edges of his jacket further around his body, angry at the reaction she so carelessly extorted from him.

Looking back from the doorway, he tried to find her in the crowd and there she was, taller than most of the other women present and graceful. Her bones were small, the thinness in her arms giving the impression of a dancer. The dark-blue gown she wore with a froth of lace at the neckline emphasised the colour in her eyes.

'Hell.' He swore and as if on cue Jonathon Wigmore, the Earl of St Ives, joined him.

'Is it the swarm of admirers around your wife you do not like, Alderworth? You might need to get used to that, for since her return to London last year every man with any sense has courted her. Lord Edmund Coleridge, of all the swains, has been the most constant fixture. She allows him more of her time than any other. We all thought you were gone, you see.'

'So you were amongst her ranks of admirers, too?'

'Indeed I was, though with little success, I might add. Her brothers are ruthless in the protection of their sister.'

For the first time since arriving back in England Tay smiled and meant it. He had something to thank Asher, Taris and Cristo Wellingham for, after all.

'There was always something damn fine about Lucinda Wellingham. I could never understand why you left when you did.'

'I was twenty-five and foolish.'

'And now?'

'Now I am older and wiser.'

The first notes of the next dance made it hard to hear and Tay watched as his wife was handed into a quadrille by Coleridge, the look on his face suggesting that he was escorting a rare and valued treasure. He looked away as her hand rested upon his shoulder and she allowed him a closeness that was improper.

Deceit came in a beautiful package with every appearance of veracity. He recalled his entrapment by the Wellinghams with an anger that was as raw as it had been all those years before.

Turning, he left the house and hailed a hansom carriage for he had not bothered with his own. Habit, he supposed, and the habitual saving of pennies even though he could now afford any number of carriages that he wished. Sitting back on the seat, he closed his eyes, the quiet noise of the hooves of the horses echoing in the street.

His wife was beautiful. But it was something else

that he saw in her pale-blue eyes. Sorrow lingered there now, the sort of sorrow that had been the hallmark of his childhood: fear overlaid with caution. It did not suit her, this new wariness, this vigilant and all-encompassing apprehension.

Breathing out hard, he cursed the Wellingham brothers their heavy-handedness, but at least, according to Jonathon Wigmore, they had kept Lucinda safe. Tay knew if he was to have any chance of successfully taking his wife to his own estate he would need to get one of them, even begrudgingly, upon his side.

Taris was the one he would target. The middle brother would not grab him in a headlock and try to pummel the daylights out of him with his failing sight and he was tired of defending himself physically every time he came into their company.

A group of women standing on a street corner beckoned to him through the window, the sort of women who had been two a penny in the gold-mining towns of Georgia. Good women some of them, with hard-luck stories almost the same as his own. There was not much to separate success from ill fortune and he had never been a man to judge another's way of dealing with the varied hands that life dealt.

He had always felt alone. Right from the first moment of perceiving that his parents saw him as a nuisance rather than a blessing and had sent him off to anyone who would have him, little care taken in making certain of the reliability and soundness of their protection. He would never bring his own children up the way his parents had him. He would love them and cherish and honour them.

He laughed to himself, although there was no humour in the sound. The heirs he hoped for were poised precariously between his wife's hatred and her brothers' aversion.

He suddenly and sincerely wished that everything could just have been easy.

Lucinda had seen Taylen Ellesmere walk for the door in the company of Jonathon Wigmore some five minutes ago.

All she wished to do was to leave, to run from the farce and close the door against gossip. But to do so would be adding to it and so she stayed, her conversation amenable and her smile bright. Only Posy watched her with any idea of the truth and she made a point not to look in the direction of her best friend at all.

Tonight she was the woman she had fostered so diligently to appear to be since she had arrived here a year before. Poised. Mannered. In such armour she was left alone, the figure of pity waiting plaintively for a husband who she thought would never return diminished into the new persona.

And now he had returned, taller and more imposing, striding into her life as if he had not left it and demanding the production of an heir. As she bit down on her disbelief, the reality of all she had agreed to seemed far more terrible without him here in front of her, yet in the recesses of places she had long since neglected a sense of excitement moved.

She would lie with him for all the long hours of the night. Had he not said so himself? A half-formed smile lifted her lips, and when Edmund Coleridge came to claim a dance she curtsied prettily and allowed him her hand.

Later as Lucinda lay in bed she replayed the conversation she had had with Taylen Ellesmere over and over in her mind.

He had promised her the freedom of deciding the time that they would lie together and he had also promised that she would enjoy it.

Such arrogance was something she would normally find most unappealing, but with Taylen Ellesmere there was a certain truth that saved him from sounding smug. Besides, when he had danced with her at the Croxleys' ball the touch of his skin against her own had made her feel…excited. Excited for the first time in years, the vibrating possibility of it all leaving her breathless.

He did not wish for a quick tumble, either, but had stipulated the promise of a whole night. It was not some momentary and sordid tryst that he was proposing, but the vow of a lengthy coupling that was…unimaginable. She was beyond the first flush of youth and had never known the things that he spoke of. A sad statement of fact, but true. Pushing back the sheets, she took off her nightgown and wandered across to the mirror on the far wall of her room.

She was not a siren with her small breasts and thinness, but everything looked to be in place, did it not? Turning to one side, she tried to make her stomach extend outwards by arching her back so that an impression of fullness was gained. What would it feel like to hold a child inside her? His child? One hand fell to the curve and she smiled and straightened, her hair falling away from her body in a long and pale curtain. Taylen was probably used to experienced, curvaceous women, women who knew what to do to make a man feel…more than she could. How would she compare to them? The smile on her face was lost.

A knock on the door had her scrambling for her nightdress and dressing gown.

Emerald walked in as she called out for her to enter and her sister-in-law did not look pleased. The conversation they had had when she had come home, she supposed, and the discussion about her intentions of joining Taylen Ellesmere.

'You do not need to leave with him, Lucy. I would bet my life on the fact that Alderworth is bluffing and if you call it he will be forced to back down completely.

'Ellesmere is not a man you can play with, Lucinda. He reminds me of the sailors on the *Mariposa*: harsh, raw men with blood on their hands and childhoods that have crushed any kindness from them. He is worse than your brothers.'

'He is not a pirate, Emerald. He is a Duke.'

'The difference only of a title. If he wants something, he will get it. I hope that thing is not you, for if he hurts one hair on your body I will—'

Lucinda interrupted her. 'I am married, Emerald, and I want to know what that feels like. I want a child and I want a home that is mine.'

'This one is yours.'

'No. It is Asher's, a ducal residence that is passed down across the generations to the next inheritor of the title. I do not wish to still be here when I am thirty and that is not far away.'

Unexpectedly Emerald began to laugh. 'Asher is hardly sleeping for the worry of what will happen and here you are actually wanting what it is he thinks you do not. Do you love Alderworth?'

'I barely know him.'

'But you are happy to take the chance of doing so?'

'Yes.'

Silence reverberated around the chamber for one long moment and then two. 'I wish to give you something.' Emerald reached into the bodice of her nightdress and slipped a necklace from around her throat. 'I have no more use for this, Lucy, but I swear that it is a formidable talisman.' She placed the green jade carving in Lucinda's outstretched hand. 'For happiness,' she explained. 'An old woman in Jamaica gifted it to me and I rarely take it off. But I want you to have it now because in wearing it I will feel that you are safe.'

Lucinda's fingers closed around the treasure still warm from Emerald's skin. 'A well-paid-for heir' did not quite seem in the spirit of the happiness the jade was imbued with, but she said nothing.

'And one more thing, Lucy. Men are simple, remember that, and you will know exactly what to do to please them.'

In the light of the candles with her hair down and her turquoise eyes bright with promise, Emerald had the look of an enchantress from one of the story books of Lucinda's childhood.

'Simple?'

'Happy with small pleasures. Sex. Food. And love if it is honest.'

Which mine is not. She almost said it, but didn't, choosing instead to slip the necklace over her head and position it above the warmth of her heart.

Taylen met Taris Wellingham at the pub of the Three Jolly Butchers in Warwick Lane and was glad when Lucinda's brother dismissed his servant to another, distant table on his arrival. He had sent the note to Taris after breakfast, hardly daring that he might heed it.

'Thank you for coming. I know it is short notice.'

Wellingham laughed. 'The idea of meeting you in a crowded pub allayed my concerns that the engagement would become physical, Alderworth. Words, however, can have the same effect of wrapping their meaning around your throat and squeezing.'

'Free speech in the broadest sense of the term?' Tay could not help but feel a certain respect for the man's intellect as he replied.

'Exactly. What is it you need?'

'I have asked your sister to come with me to Alderworth Manor tomorrow, and she has agreed.'

'You have asked her already?'

'Last night at the Croxleys' ball. She has agreed.'

'Then there must have been a strong reward to entice her to such a promise. She is not apt to sing your praises about anything.'

Disconcerting opaque eyes watched him with all the focus of one who could see to the heart of the matter clearly.

'Lucinda hates you. How plain do you need to hear it in order to go away, Alderworth, or are you one of those obtuse men who fancy they see hope where there is none and would batter their heads against a brick wall for the rest of their days rather than facing a truth they do not wish to hear?'

'Going away is no longer an option for me.' Tay kept his voice low. 'Lucinda is my wife according to the letter of the law and under the authority of the Church, and I would never agree to a divorce. Besides, I have enough money to care for her now and the desire to do so.'

'Desire?' Unexpectedly Wellingham leant forwards and one hand shot out to entrap his in a grasp that was unyielding. A surprising accuracy, too, given his lack of sight. 'Desire to bed our sister again and then leave her? Desire to beget an heir upon her and then be on your way into the shady corners of the world when nothing turns out quite as easy as you expected it to? That kind of desire?'

Had his wife already spoken to her brothers about their bargain? Surely not. His hand ached with the force of strong fingers wrapped into flesh, but he did not pull away. Let the bastard see how little anyone could ever hurt him again. Aye, Taris Wellingham could break every damn bone in his hand and he would allow himself no reaction.

And then Lucinda's brother let go, simply sitting back against the fine leather chair and lifting his glass to drink as if nothing had happened.

'My *desire* to protect your sister is none of your business, Lord Wellingham.' Taylen did not make any effort to accord the words politeness, scrawling them instead with the seedy innuendo her brother had read into their meaning.

The show of force from the older man was a smokescreen. He could do nothing legally to stop them leaving and he knew it. Threading his hands in his lap to prevent himself from retaliation, Tay waited. This meeting was not going anything like he had hoped that it would.

'With a name slathered and immured in depravity, it might be hard to protect anyone or anything, Alderworth. Your history of wildness and debauchery does not make for good reading and a hundred men and women of the *ton* would swear you are the Devil incarnate. No.' He shook his head. 'If we are looking into the etymology of words, I doubt *protection* in your book has the same meaning as it does in mine.'

The stubborn anger in Lucinda's brother's voice was more than evident—a man who was at the end of his tether and showing it. Taking in a breath, Tay took a different tack. 'Does Carisbrook know you have met me here this morning?'

'He does. His instructions were to stick a knife through the place where your heart should be.'

'Explicit.'

'Very.'

Tay detected the beginnings of a smile. 'Then perhaps we could forge a bargain that might suit us all.'

'Indeed?' The tone was not encouraging, but he needed to get at least one of the Wellinghams on his side and he had long admired Taris.

'I propose that my wife continues to reside in your family's town house for the next few weeks on the condition that I can escort her to various public functions of her choosing. That will allow you to see that I am not as black as you might paint me and give her time to see that I am not the bastard she thinks I am.'

'Asher has control of Lucinda's assets and all of her money.'

'Good.'

'And you will get none of it.'

His words were bland, no true reflection at all of the topic under discussion.

'All I want is a chance.'

'I can promise nothing without talking to my sister. I will, however, be advising her to run as fast and far away from you as she can and to refuse to partake in further dialogue or to accept other correspondence. If it is simply a case of enough money to be rid of you, then we have the means…'

'It isn't.'

'I thought not.'

He raised one arm and his man came immediately to his side. 'If Lucinda feels she would be interested in finding out more about the sort of man she has married, then I will not stop her and neither will my brothers. But it will be her decision, Alderworth, not yours.'

When Tay nodded and held out his hand, Taris Wellingham failed to respond. Laying his fingers upon the pristine white cloth covering the table, he stood as the other did and watched him leave, a tall dark-haired man who made his way with his servant beside him across the salon of a busy public bar, his lack of sight completely hidden to all those observing him.

Chapter Eight

'You do not have to go to this ball with Alderworth, Lucy. We can fight any allegation he might make through the courts and completely ruin his name.'

Taris took her hand and tears pooled behind Lucinda's eyes at both the familiarity and the safety.

'The Church recognises the sanctity of holy marriage and Taylen Ellesmere made it clear that he would never agree to a divorce.'

'Then let us talk to him again…'

'No.' She was most adamant about that. There was nothing more to be said. The Duke of Alderworth had offered her a proposition and freedom looked admirable after years of being shackled to a missing husband. All her friends, save Posy, were married and bearing children whilst she had wilted, growing old upon a shelf of her own making, withering into someone she had never thought to become.

She could bear it no longer, this middle land of no

choice at all, and, standing here in her best dress of light-blue shot silk, she knew that she wanted more.

'I need the chance to understand the only husband I am ever likely to have.'

She did not tell Taris that she had never been the slightest bit attracted to any other suitor in all her years of being out in society or that there was something about Taylen Ellesmere that made her heart run faster. She did not say that his green eyes had a promise in them she had found shocking because of her own capacity for response or that when he had spoken of the things he might like to do with her body at the Croxleys' ball she had finally felt...aroused.

Beatrice, from her place on the other side of the room, joined in the conversation.

'You are sure that this is what you wish, Lucinda? Alderworth seems both dangerous and alarming, a man who might be hard to tame.'

'He is my legal husband, Bea.'

'Your husband of only a few hours.' Her sister-in-law's voice was tight, though beneath it lurked a tone that was surprising. If Lucinda could have named it, she might have chanced humour.

Taris interceded. 'If there is ever any danger and you feel...'

'I am going to a ball a half a mile from home, Taris, with hundreds of people I know all around me. How could that possibly be dangerous?'

'Alderworth will not come here to get you?'

She shook her head. 'He said he would wait for

me at the Chesterfields' in Audley Street because he does not wish for another contretemps. Every time one of you meet him someone has been hurt so I can well understand his point.'

'Then I will ask you to give him this.' He pulled a letter from his pocket sealed in an envelope. Looking over at Beatrice, Lucinda knew the pair must have fashioned the missive last night when she had returned with the news of her imminent departure, a plan that had been changed that very morning to include at least two weeks in London.

'What is in it?'

'A warning. If Alderworth does anything to hurt you, anything at all, Asher, Cris and I will hunt him down to the very edges of the earth.' He swiped one hand through his hair, pushing back the darkness and looking as angry as she had ever seen him.

Goodness, if her brothers had any inkling of the agreement she had consented to regarding the conception of an heir, she doubted that they would have sent only a note.

The Chesterfield town house was one of the prettiest in Mayfair and one of the grandest, too, the sweeping drive of white pebbles leading to an imposing portico. Two men in livery stood at attention at each side of the wide flight of steps, Taylen Ellesmere between them, the darkness of his attire in complete contrast to the bright scarlet jackets they sported. He came forwards as he saw her and opened the door of her carriage, gesturing the Chesterfield servants away and shepherding her down a side path lit with lanterns, where they were hidden by trees.

Tonight he was dressed in charcoal, his long-tailed coat and breeches of the best-quality superfine. His cravat was loosely tied, no artifice in it, the snowy white of the fabric showing up the darkness of his skin and hair. A tall man and graceful with it. Where he touched her arm she felt the heat of contact. The ring she had given him all those years ago lay on his wedding finger and the small spark of recognition made her feel warmer. She was sure he had not been wearing it yesterday.

'I did not think you would come.' Lucinda could smell strong drink on his breath as he turned and stopped.

'I have a message for you.' In his company tonight she felt…uncertain and she hated the fact that she did. But in a crowded ballroom she knew she could simply slip away if she needed to. The thought calmed her as he turned the envelope over and looked closely at the writing. Breaking the seal, he opened the letter, reading it quickly before handing it back to her. 'This concerns you.'

Alderworth. One wrong move with our sister and you will pay for it.

The message was unsigned, but the parchment had the Wellingham insignia emblazoned at the top, an eagle argent on sable.

'You are fortunate in your protection.' His voice was an echo of some lost thing, surprising her.

'My brothers have been the most wonderful support in the world but…I am tired of being for ever thankful.'

Sacrilege to even utter such a sentiment, but she did, the words running into the silence between them like sharp daggers. Taking a breath, she looked around her at the other carriages coming up the drive. She was glad for the privacy the trees here afforded them.

'And the proposition I gave you yesterday?'

'You said you would not rush me, your Grace.' This time she looked directly at him, catching his eyes with her own in challenge.

'So formal?'

'We are strangers, you and I, who have been tied by the binding agreement of a marriage that is to neither of our liking. I barely know anything of you.'

'Which might be a good thing,' he returned, his words overlaid with just a tinge of regret. It was enough for Lucinda to press her conditions further.

'I couldn't tolerate the sort of parties you have made famous. An endless list of drunken guests parading through the places I reside within would be abhorrent to me and until…'

She could not finish because he leant forwards to take her hand, stroking the palm with his thumb so that small *frissons* of desire ran in ever-increasing strength up her arm.

'Until you are ripe with child?'

The shocking reality of the words made her pull back. That she could even have thought to control a man like Taylen Ellesmere, whose very world was so far from her own, was naïve.

'You may well laugh at our situation, your Grace, but I know that you accepted a large sum of money from my brother to disappear for ever. It is hard to trust a groom who only thinks to profit substantially from his bride.'

He looked away, a muscle in the side of his neck rippling with the tension only the guilty could feel. Asher had told her last night of the enormity of the sum Tay Ellesmere had taken and for a moment she had thought to rescind every agreement between them completely. But she had not. *Why* was a notion she found difficult to fathom, the thought of being tied to a man who had gained much fiscally from her misery more than demeaning. Lucinda waited for him to explain, to find some honour in his actions and clarify his reasons, but he stayed silent.

She felt the breaking of hope almost as a pain.

He was greedy and he was reckless. He was also dangerous, distant and intimidating. But there lay beneath the image he showed to the world other shadows, too, quieter and more beguiling. Tragedy was one such veil. She had seen it once when he had spoken of his uncle.

Secrets and silence stretched between them, the

sound of the world around distant, though her heart-beat drummed at a frantic rhythm in her ears.

He could not bring himself to say he had paid her brother back each and every single penny twofold, penance for the only time in his life where his integrity had been held to ransom. Not now. That would come later, far away from accusation and dishonour and the reality of an enticement he had succumbed to in desperation.

Breathing out hard, he tried to take a stock of things. His estranged wife looked a little like his mother used to, beautiful and prickly and angling for a fight, wanting high emotion to wreck what little peace he had left.

God. Patricia Ellesmere had used every single second of her life to make it harder for those near her and as her son it had often been him. Tay did not want acrimony and argument. He did not want greed and wrongdoing to punctuate everything that he was now, leaching out contentment and serenity.

Had he made a huge mistake by coming back after all, searching for an elusive something he could not quite forget? Almost three years of separation had hardened Lucinda. He could see it in her eyes. She was a different woman now, less innocent, more worldly.

'If it is of any use, I would apologise for the way I left. Excuses can only go a certain way in the alleviation of great pain so I won't bore you with them.'

'I have not heard even one explanation as yet, your Grace.' Her blue eyes were reflected in the silk of her dress, almost a match in colour.

'The dukedom was bankrupt.'

Surprise crept across her face. 'Surely my brother did not promise to rescue the Alderworth estate in its entirety?'

'No. He gave me the chance to do that myself. I hit a rich seam of gold in a river at the foot of the North Georgia mountains and had the luck to sell my claim for a tidy sum. After that I invested in the only services on a gold field that truly raise capital, the transportation facilities. The fortunes in mining are random, you see, but the large profits in the adjoining industries are not.'

'So you have arrived home rich?'

'I have.'

'And because of it you feel the need of an heir.'

He nodded.

'An unbroken line?'

'Precisely.'

'The saying that one person's luck is another's misfortune comes to mind.' Her mouth was a single tight line of fury.

She spoke as the forgotten wife who was suddenly recalled for duty a thousand days after he had left her. Such a thought was sobering, the contract for an heir stretching between them.

'If there is someone else who has gained your affections whilst I have been away, then I would—'

She did not let him finish. 'There isn't.'

Tay could not even begin to understand the relief he felt at her answer.

'After…us…I was largely left alone by others. Ruin has its own particular brand of isolation that is not easy to shake off. Besides, your reputation for debauchery and sexual experience meant all were wary.'

'When did you return to London?'

'Last year. My brothers insisted on it and their influence paved my way. It was all going well until…'

'I came back.'

She nodded and looked aside.

'Why, then, did you agree to come with me?'

He thought for a moment that she might not answer, as her eyes flinted in anger, but then she did, her voice shaking. 'Because anything is better than the stigma of abandonment.'

'I should not have let your brothers threaten me. I should have stayed and taken you to my home.'

'And forfeited your gold?' Her tone was neither soft nor conciliatory. It was hard and biting. 'No, your Grace, your promised largesse will go a long way in allowing me the freedom of a future I want.'

Tay shifted his stance and looked at her closely. She made him feel like the low-life he had not been, her lies cornering him into defending himself before her brothers, the licentious duke who had ruined a favoured sister.

Only he hadn't.

He had bundled up a woman who, with little persuasion, would have been easy to bed, but instead he had ordered a carriage and driven her home.

He had been paying for it ever since, by God, because the Wellinghams bore a grudge with great persistence, even one based on deceit.

He had sent his own correspondence, too, of course, a few careful letters explaining his daily routines and the harsh beauty of the countryside around Dahlonega. His wife had never written back. Not once. Tay wondered if Cristo Wellingham had stayed true to his promise and delivered the notes.

He could ask her, he supposed, pull the truth out of lies, but he had no more stomach for it and an idea hatched in the lonely fields of American dreams made little sense here.

The brothers' latest missive sizzled in his hand full of threat, the careful illusions of their wedding day dissolved here into only disappointment.

For them both.

'When we go to Alderworth Manor you will be given your own suite of rooms. I shall not presume on you for anything save for the fulfilment of our bargain.'

He turned away as she nodded and felt his body respond in anticipation of all that was implied.

I shall not presume on you for anything save for the fulfillment of our bargain.

A duty that had turned into obligation, the giving of her body for a sum of money and the promise of future freedom. A chore and a task that sounded onerous tonight. Lucinda couldn't decide just where she had lost all sense of herself: at Alderworth Manor three years ago or here, hurtling towards her marital requirements, only a womb for rent.

She could find no common ground with a husband who was a stranger, forged in hatred and anger by a family that gave no credence to close bonds or honest discourse.

'If I come, I would need at least a few weeks to settle in.' She blurted the words out, each one running on top of the other in a stream of quickness. 'I could not just be...'

She found it hard to finish.

'Pounced upon?'

Humour laced the query and she was glad for it, but still she pressed on.

'I would also require some sort of kindness, your Grace.'

This time he did laugh. 'How many men have you slept with, Lady Lucinda?' He did not use her married name and she did not answer. The corded arteries in his throat were raised in the dim light.

'I realise, of course, that you are used to faster women, women who would think nothing of sharing around their charms and making certain every man got their portion, but I am not of that ilk, your Grace, and if you think that I might change...'

'I do not wish for that at all.'

'Oh.' All of the wind went from her sails and she stood there, exposed and waiting. 'I need at least a few weeks,' she repeated, the quiver in her demand easily heard. Should she have bargained for more time? A month. A year?

'Very well.' His voice was hoarse, a promise co-erced only under duress. When he turned and offered her his arm, she could do nothing other than take it as he walked her back to the portico. Joining other couples who made their way up the wide staircase, the light from the lamps showed up his face as a handsome and distant mask.

Lucinda had not understood just exactly what it meant to be at the side of a man who was the most vilified and envied Duke in all of London. When their names were called as they stood waiting to go in, she heard the distinct murmur of surprise and a momentary lull in conversation of the three hundred or so guests present.

'The Duke and Duchess of Alderworth.'

'Notoriety has its own set of drawbacks and this is one of them.' His voice was soft and steady, not a care in the world showing as he smiled at those who might crucify him. 'Let us just hope that your unblemished pedigree shelters you from some of it.'

'With an attitude like that it is a wonder you still receive invitations to anything at all, your Grace,' she replied.

'No one wants to be the first to leave the lofty

ducal title off their guest list and especially now they know all the coffers are full.'

'How full?'

The tone in his voice changed somewhat as he replied. 'Full enough to call in the chits of men with fewer morals than I have.' As she pulled back he made an effort to lighten such darkness. 'Full enough so that you could order as many gowns as you desire and I would barely notice, Duchess.'

'Tempting.'

His hand closed tighter in a movement that claimed her as his wife and Lucinda was pleased not one of her brothers was present as they walked down into the crowd. Edmund Coleridge was at the front of the group and smiled at her fondly, but she did not encourage him to come forwards because a small part of her worried that Alderworth would slice any tenderness to pieces should he know of it.

The Beauchamps, Lord Daniel and his French wife Lady Camille, were the first to receive them.

'I had heard you were back, Tay. How long are you here for?'

His brown eyes were kind and Camille Beauchamp seemed just as welcoming. Perhaps this evening would not be as difficult as Lucinda had thought it, her husband's reputation melding with her own to produce some sort of a halfway point of acceptability.

'Only a few weeks.'

'Then you might come to see us before then.' Camille joined the conversation for the first time, her lilting French accent beautiful. 'My husband made a point of telling me that you speak French well, your Grace. I should enjoy a conversation in my native language.'

More couples drifted over towards them, amongst the group an old school friend of Lucinda's. Annabelle Browne was as effusive as ever.

'Why, I just absolutely cannot imagine what it must have been like for your husband to have spent three years in the Americas, Lucy. My brother, Anthony, was in Washington for only a small amount of time and he was most forthcoming about the primitive state of the place.'

'I suspect that Alderworth managed,' she returned.

'The gold fields were dens of iniquity, I am told. It was a shame you could not have been there with him, to guide him through the pitfalls.'

'Oh, I am certain my husband was able to navigate them by himself, Annabelle.' The cutting she had received from Annabelle's brother came to mind and in an effort to change the topic she looked around at the others present. But Annabelle Browne was as persistent as she was dull-witted.

'Tony says the Duke was lucky in his windfall and that he left Georgia under a cloud.'

'A cloud of what?'

'Suspicion. His partner in the mining venture, Montcrieff, was killed and there was some discussion as to who would have benefitted most from such a tragedy. It seems Alderworth did.' She smiled sweetly, setting Lucinda's teeth on an edge.

'I am certain had there been anything untoward, the constabulary would have moved in.'

'But they did, you see, that is my very point. Tony said that your Duke was supposed to come before the courts in Atlanta, but—'

She stopped, aware of Alderworth's glance upon her.

'I was freed, Miss Browne, as an innocent man. The law has its uses after all, even though most of the time it is an ass.' His smile was languid, the creases in his cheeks deep against his tan and in a room full of men who had spent the good part of the day getting ready for this evening's entertainment he looked untamed—a ranging wolf amongst dainty chickens. The vibrant green of his eyes added to his menace.

Annabelle turned red and for a moment Lucinda viewed the world as Taylen might have, the innuendo and aspersion on his character a constant presence. She made herself smile as she faced her husband.

'It is most trying when people insist on passing on false rumours, do you not think, Duke?'

'Indeed,' he returned, and they both watched as the woman gave her goodbyes and dragged the man she was with away.

'I do not need you to defend me,' he said as Annabelle Browne moved out of hearing and the anger in his voice was sharp.

'Do you not, your Grace? I should have thought the very opposite.' She stood her ground as he loomed above her.

'Doubts begin to creep in if one crows one's innocence too loudly, I find.' He was back to his most infuriating best.

'It is more than doubts that hold those in this room enthralled in the saga of the Alderworth family. Were I to name it I might chance…fear.'

A small flicker of doubt came into his face. 'Do you fear me then, too?'

'No.' Surprisingly she did not. The answer tripped from her tongue in truth as their glances met and held, a living flame of heat that curled around sense and wisdom. She should fear him because every single thing she heard about him compromised all she had known before and just as they were finding a footing together some other new and terrible story pushed all accord aside leaving only this…attraction.

It would never be enough, she knew, tragedy and disaster trumping proper judgement and good sense. But she could not help it.

Intrinsically flawed.

And she was.

Lucinda was looking at him as though he might stab the next person who came to talk to them. The aspersions just aired, he supposed, as the face of Lance Montcrieff rose up in memory, an accident with their rudimentary stamp mill in Ward's Creek slicing through his thigh just below the groin.

It had taken less than ten minutes for him to bleed out, despite Tay's efforts to staunch the flow, and Tay had held his hand through every long and harrowing one of them, willing his friend to live even as breath dulled and stopped. Gold took no account of the integrity of its victims, for if it had it would have been him lying there with cold blue on his lips and death in his skin, thousands of miles from home.

Another loss. Another brush with the law. Another woman without a husband, another child fatherless.

Swallowing, he pulled himself back into the ballroom on Audley Street with its chandeliers and wide curtained alcoves, marbled pillars and liveried servants.

A gentle England that had not been his for a long, long time. He had forgotten its beauty and peace, he thought, as his wife swayed unconsciously to the beat of music, deliberately not looking his way.

'Would you dance with me again?'

He expected her to refuse, but she did not. Instead he found her fingers within his outstretched hand and then they were on the floor amongst the other couples, the music of a waltz beginning.

He had always liked the way she fitted into him, her head just under the curve of his chin, liked how she allowed him to lead her, an easy flowing dancer with a light and clever step.

He did not usually dance at these social occasions, but spent the hours in the card rooms drinking away the night.

'How did the man in America die? The one Annabelle spoke of, I mean?' Her query was soft and he could think of no other of his acquaintance who might have asked this question so directly of him.

'His name was Lance. Lance Montcrieff. We set up a stamp mill outside Dahlonega to crush the ore from the tunnels and release the gold. When the sapling holding the structure broke and it all came down on him, he never stood a chance. We were ten hours from the nearest township, you understand, and a lot of that was over rough terrain.'

'Why did they blame you?'

'Gold has the propensity to make fools of every man and a rich claim incites questions. I was the one who would profit most from his death, after all, and there was no one else about to vouch that my story was true.'

Her breath hitched against the skin at his throat. Another truth she did not want probably. Another way she would be disappointed in him.

'Trouble never seems very far away from your door, your Grace. Do you ever wonder why?'

Shaking his head, he was amazed when she let him pull her closer, their bodies now touching almost like lovers. The firm daintiness of her breasts rubbed against his chest and he pushed his groin against her own in a quiet statement of intent.

Slender fingers tightened on his hands. Their bodies talked now in the smallest of caresses, almost accidental, never hurried—a slight pressure here, a small stroke there, too new for words, too fragile for any true acknowledgement. Taylen had never been in a room before and felt so removed from everybody in it. Save her. Save his wife with her straightforward questions and her unexpected allegiance.

'What is Edmund Coleridge to you?'

'A friend who has helped me to laugh again.'

'That is all. Just the laughter?' He did not care for the hesitation in her words or the sudden stiffness in her body.

'Why all these questions, your Grace?' She smiled as she asked, a smile that made her look so beautiful, with her deep-set dimples and pale spun-gold hair, that he had to glance away.

'My father may have had no problem with being cuckolded, Duchess, but I most certainly do.' He did not like the unease he could so plainly hear in his words.

'Three years of absence makes your insistence on celibacy rather hard to take, your Grace. Perhaps I should inform you that a woman, contrary to belief, has as many needs as a man.'

'Needs I wish to fill, sweetheart, and tonight if you would let me.'

He felt shock run down through all the parts of her body in a hot and hard wash, and was glad for it. If he had been anywhere else save in a crowded ballroom, he could have used such a reaction to persuade her to take a chance on him. Such an easy seduction. He had done it so many times before, after all, and not one woman had ever held complaint.

Yet as he gritted his teeth those faceless paramours dissolved into the ether just as they had done for a while now, lost to him and formless, lovers with the word skewered into only faithless lust. The broken promises of his childhood bound into the present.

When the music stopped they came apart and he was glad for the distance as he went to find a drink.

Lucinda felt giddy. A ridiculous word, she knew, but it explained her lack of certainty entirely. Taylen Ellesmere threw her into a place that was without compass, directionless and wanton.

Wanton? Another word she smiled at. Tonight her vocabulary regarding misdirected emotions was growing and she did not wish for it to stop. Already she looked for him across the room, tall and dark amongst a sea of others.

She was like a moth to his light, fluttering unheeded, waiting to be burnt. Her brothers had warned her, her sisters-in-law had told her stories about him and none of the tales had been kind. Yet still some invisible bond drew her to him, the wedding ring circling her finger a part of it, but nowhere near the total. Her nails dug into the soft flesh of her palms as she pondered her intentions.

What did she want of him? She could not even begin to name it.

Posy Tompkins came to her side and took her hand. Lucinda liked the warm familiarity of the action.

'You look beautiful tonight, Luce, and I think that fact has something to do with the return of your mysterious husband. Edmund has already been whining to me about your lack of attention.'

'You never liked him, Posy. I am not certain why.'

'He is a boy compared to the Duke of Alderworth, a boy who in the end would disappoint you.'

'And you think that the Duke would not?'

'I think he has been misjudged by society. I think he is strong like your brothers and honourable in his way. I think, if you gave him a chance, he might surprise you.'

'You were always the romantic, Posy.'

'To find the happiness you haven't had ever since your wedding, Luce, you might need to allow Alderworth some ground for compromise, for a bending is better than a breaking. If it were me, I would grab him with both hands and never let him go.'

'Fine words from a woman who has sworn off relationships for ever.'

Posy's more normal optimism was sliced by a sadness Lucinda had sometimes seen in her friend before. 'He reminds me of a man I knew a long time ago, in Italy.'

Their conversation was interrupted by the arrival

of the Elliott twins, their voices louder than they needed to be.

'Lucinda, it is so wonderful that your husband is finally back. You must be thrilled that he has returned after all this time?'

Elizabeth Elliott was as effusive as her sister, Louise. 'Everybody is talking about him, of course, and it seems he has arrived back in England a lot richer than when he left it. Perhaps you might both come to our ball on Saturday night—for Edmund Coleridge had already said that he will be there.'

The questionable undercurrents of the *ton* at play, Lucinda thought, and was glad when Posy took charge.

'I had heard a rumour that you are to be married, Lady Elizabeth. Is it true?'

A scream of delight and then much was made of a ring on the third finger of her left hand. Lucinda scanned the room for any sign of her husband and was disappointed when she could not see him at all. Had he simply left or was he in the card room, drinking himself into oblivion and losing a fortune? The excitement she had felt before was suddenly changed into cold hard worry and she did not like the feeling at all.

Ten minutes later she made her way to a large terrace overlooking the garden and was about to walk out on to the edge of it when a scuffle and shouting at the far end caught her attention. Richard Allenby, the Earl of Halsey, was pummelling someone on the ground, a number of others around the prone body adding their particular attentions. Turning away in order to find somebody to help, she saw the profile of the person they were hurting suddenly in the light.

'Taylen.' Shouting, she moved forwards, catching the group unawares, each one of them looking towards her with a varying degree of disbelief on their faces. Then she was amongst them, sheltering her husband with her body and daring them to go through her person to get to him.

Blood was on his nose and his chin, a long cut across the back of his head and a metal bar lying down beside him. He looked groggy and dazed, his collar crooked and his jacket torn.

'You have no business here.' Allenby's voice. She turned to face him with pure wrath.

'No business, Lord Halsey?' Her hand came out to push him back. 'Will you hit me next, then? Do you creep up on defenceless women as well as men?' She stooped as she spoke; her fingers found the bar and she raised it above her head. 'If anyone comes closer, I will use it on them and I will scream the place down as I do it, you understand. And then when people come running I will tell them exactly what I saw; a bunch of cowardly thugs beating up a badly injured, half-conscious man in their midst and enjoying it.'

Silence reigned except for the breath of her husband, taken noisily through blood and mucus, then they were gone, all of them, the door to the ballroom shutting, leaving them alone.

She leant down to him, his blood staining her blue silk as she tried to mop up his face with her hem. Her hands shook with the shock of it all and she made an effort to still them.

She knew the moment he came back into full consciousness because he stiffened and tried to stand, coming up to his haunches in a way that suggested great pain and swaying with the movement.

'The bastards hit me from behind.' His fingers worked around into his hair, finding a gash as he looked at the bar. 'They used that, I suppose. Halsey always was a coward.'

Lucinda thought that his pupils looked larger than they should be, green shrunk into darkness. He blinked a lot, too, as though his vision was impaired and he was trying to find the way to correct it.

'There are stairs at the other end of the terrace. If we went through the garden, we could get to the road to find your carriage.'

'You would come with me?'

'Of course I would. You need help.'

'If people see us, they will talk.'

When she laughed it felt free and real and good, a surprising discovery with the trauma of all that was happening around her. 'They talk now, your Grace, and there is too much blood to go back into the ballroom. If they see you like this, everything will be worse.'

Nodding, he came up into a standing position, though his hands used the balustrade to steady himself, to find his balance. 'I have ruined your gown.' His top lip was thickening even as he spoke.

'A small consideration given all of the others.'

The music had begun again, calling those present to the dancing, and Lucinda was pleased for it. With so much happening inside it would be far less likely for a guest to take the air on the terrace. Placing her arm across his, she led him down the steps, the small pathways amongst the plants lined with white chip stone which made it easy to traverse in the moonlight. Before a moment or so had passed they were out at the gate and Lucinda hailed the Alderworth conveyance, which languished further down the road, the driver throwing a cheroot to the ground and stomping it underfoot before climbing up into the driving box.

Another moment and they were inside with the door closed behind them and, for the first time since finding her husband at the feet of his assailants, Lucinda took in an easy breath. They would not be discovered like this, battered and bloodied after such a scandalous attack. They were safe.

Reaching into her reticule, she found a handkerchief. 'Here, let me help you.'

His hand came out as he shook away the offer, anger evident in his refusal.

'Why would Halsey waylay you in the way he did?'

Taylen Ellesmere raised his head slightly and had the temerity to smile.

'Because, once upon a time, I did just the same to him.'

Chapter Nine

'You crept up on him like a coward and knocked him out?'

He shook his head and then clutched at the side of it.

'With a whole group of others to help you do your dirty work?'

'Of course not.'

'You used an iron bar on his scalp and hit him with it from behind, allowing him no chance to defend himself, and when he was down you kicked at his face?'

He seemed to suddenly lose patience with her questions, leaning forwards to take her hand into his.

'Thank you, Lucinda.'

'You are welcome, Taylen.'

His blood had made his palm sticky and he was careful to wipe her fingers with the tail of his shirt when he let go. Such a simple action and so much imbued within it. She looked away so that he would not see the emotion on her face. Outside the London streets were as busy as usual, nothing changed. Inside her world had shifted, though, the touch of his fingers against her own different now, more familiar. His smell. His warmth. The breadth of his thighs as they pressed against the velour on the seat.

'My parents always believed in the concept of treating everyone as an enemy. Tonight I forgot.' The words were said concisely, as if he would place a point on each one of them.

'Advice like that makes me wonder whether such people have the right to offspring. Surely no child deserves to be brought up under such a cruel misconception.'

The sound of his laughter filled the small space, allowing accord to push through shock and anger. 'Are you usually so forthright, Duchess?'

'Indeed I am, Duke. My family would tell you that it is one of my greatest faults.'

His head shook as the Wellingham town house came into view, the action shadowed on the wall of the carriage behind him by the light from the portico. His hair had worked free from its leather strap and lay around his shoulders, darker than the darkness.

'But I would not. Free speech has always been a particular preference of mine. I think it a residue of being raised by parents who never said what they actually thought.'

'Because they were trying to protect you?'

He laughed again and was about to say something more when a movement on the stairs before them caught his attention. 'It seems we have a welcoming party.'

Lucinda's heart sank. With the blood from his nose still smeared across his face, a rapidly darkening eye and a thickened lip, Taylen Ellesmere looked exactly like the reprobate her brothers had good reason to think that he was.

'I won't come in. I doubt my body could take another beating.' The dispassionate and cynical Duke was back, no warmth in his eyes at all as the footman opened the door and the light spilled upon them.

'A further rowdy night of fighting, Alderworth?' Asher's question was layered with disgust.

'Someone has to subdue the scum of London. It may as well be me.'

'No, it isn't as you think it—' Lucinda began as she stepped down from the coach, but her husband cut her off.

'I will see you tomorrow, Duchess. Thank you for the most interesting of evenings.'

A rap with his cane on the roof had the horses moving, the perfectly matched pair of greys gathering speed as they disappeared down the road.

'His blood has ruined your gown.' Asher ground the words out as they walked back inside.

'Halsey did it. Halsey and a group of his cowardly friends. They caught him alone on the terrace at the ball in a planned attack. He had no chance against them.'

A look crossed her brother's face, dark and unexplainable, and a terrible idea suddenly occurred to Lucinda.

'You did not pay anyone to do that to him, did you, Ashe?'

'Halsey is a weak-willed and arrogant sycophant. If I wanted the job done, I would do it properly myself.'

'Well, don't.' She stood to her tallest height in her stained and crumpled gown, the shock of the evening on her face and an anger boiling beneath everything that was dubious. 'Hurt Alderworth, I mean. I am tired of being the forgotten wife and I want at least the chance to…' She stopped, not quite able to voice what it was she did want.

'The chance to what?' His dark eyes were filled with an urgent question.

'To…know something of the man I have married.'

With that she swept past, making for the staircase and the privacy of her room.

Tay held a hand close against his chest. He was sure a few of his ribs were broken and knew they would hurt like the devil in the morning. Breathing shallowly, he leaned forwards, finding in the movement a slight relief. The wedding ring he had retrieved that morning from the bottom drawer of his library desk felt solid on his finger.

Lucinda had seen him helpless at the feet of a pack of cowards who had crept up on him as he was lighting a cheroot, the evening with his wife making him less vigilant than he normally was. Usually the *ton* avoided any contretemps or whiff of scandal, but Lucinda had come forwards with her integrity and her honour, admonishing grown men with words that he could not have bettered.

Like a fierce and urgent angel. Lord, he was the sinner married to a saint and with his past it would be her paying for such loyalty again and again and again. The shock in her eyes, her trembling fingers, her ruined gown and disappointment scrawled in deep lines across her brow. He had seen her stiffen when her oldest brother had come out to meet them. Another mortification. He smiled at the word and then regretted it as the skin on his top lip stung.

Without Lucinda here everything hurt, badly, a cold emptiness closing in about him. He would not meet her tomorrow or the day after that, for he needed time to nurse his wounds and to try to find some idea as to where to go to next.

He could not keep putting his wife into danger or see her compromised by his own lack of regard for the law and there were more of the ilk of Halsey out there than he would have liked to admit.

Remembering Lucinda's words in the carriage as she had tried to explain to him why he was nothing like Richard Allenby, he smiled. No one had ever been on his side before, not like that and in the face of such damning evidence. The feeling was… warming.

Shaking his head hard, he told himself to put such nonsense aside. Twenty-eight years had taught him a few home truths and one of them was to depend upon nobody.

Treat everyone as an enemy.

His mother and father's son after all, the words scrawled into his flesh like a tattoo. Ineradicable and permanent.

Lucinda did not see Taylen Ellesmere the next day or the day after. No note of explanation came.

Her brothers had ceased to talk of Alderworth whatsoever, hoping perhaps that by ignoring him he might go away, but she haunted the wide front-window bays like a wraith, glancing out each time a noise caught her attention or the sound of hooves echoed on the street, her breath catching with every newcomer turning into the square, eyes picking out their livery with interest. He might be laying low, but the bargain for an heir that they had struck between them still simmered underneath everything, calling through the silence.

'You seem jumpy.' Eleanor sat on the small sofa in the blue room working on a tapestry.

Smiling half-heartedly, Lucinda picked up her own needlework, but the stitches blurred before her, the counting of each one difficult today.

'I did not sleep well last night or the one before

that.' Goodness, that was an understatement. She had lain awake almost till the dawn, worrying.

'I could make you one of my tonics if you like. It is bound to help you relax.'

As Lucinda shook her head to decline the offer, the needle pierced her finger, drawing blood, yet instead of wiping it away she watched as the red of the wound spread into white cotton. Other blood came to mind. The injuries Taylen Ellesmere had sustained were substantial and damaging and she wondered how he fared now. Who would tend to him and make certain he was not becoming worse? His breathing had been laboured, after all, and she was sure his nose had been broken.

Standing again, she walked to the window, unconcerned as to what Eleanor might make of her distractedness. Outside drizzle coated the world in grey, a few leaves falling on the gardens with their ragged yellow edges brittle. Like her. She felt the tension in all of the corners of her body, scraping away contentment, panic close to the skin. Tears pooled at the back of her eyes. One step forwards and then two steps back. She was tired of the uncertainty and the confusion.

'Is the contretemps at the Chesterfield ball worrying you?' Eleanor came to stand beside Lucinda, the palm of her hand making contact.

A nod brought the hand fully around Lucinda's shoulders.

'Cristo thinks Alderworth may have been the one

to deal with Halsey three years ago, which would explain the attack upon him in Mayfair after the carriage accident. He said that he may have misjudged him.'

'Alderworth would not thank him for the compliment were he to hear of it, Eleanor.'

'Because he is prickly and distant and completely unmindful of a reputation that is hardly salutary? Or because he likes to hide behind an image that is not entirely the truth?' The tone in her words was a worried one. 'His grandmother used to hit him, you know. Hard. She thought such training would make a man of her grandchild because her own daughter had become such a biting disappointment with her many lovers and her drinking.'

Bile rose in Lucinda's throat as she turned to her sister-in-law. 'Who told you that?'

'Rosemary Jones, my maid's older sister. She works at Falder now, but as a young girl she was employed by Lady Shields at her home in Essex.'

'Many children are punished, Eleanor.'

'Not in the way he was. According to Rosemary, he spent months away from the family in a hospital in Rouen after one particular incident. Then his uncle took him away.'

'An uncle? Which uncle?'

'Hugo Shields, Lord Sutton, I think was the name mentioned. His mother's brother. Rosemary did not see any of the family again because she was asked to leave. The old lady had some inkling of her disapproval, I suppose, and did not wish to be reminded of an unsavoury period in her life.'

Goodness. The whole horror of everything began to mount inside Lucinda. Between a heavy-handed grandmother and a brutal uncle, the small Taylen Ellesmere never had a chance, just as he did not now with the building censure of a society that barely knew him.

'I think I will take the carriage out, Eleanor. I need to see my milliner about a hat.'

'I will tell your brothers that you have a few errands to do, Lucy. I know there are a pile of library books well overdue from Hookham's Lending Library if you would not mind dropping them off for me.'

'Certainly.' She smiled as Eleanor did. Both knew that the Ellesmere town house was only a few hundred yards from the mentioned establishment, a distance easy to walk.

The door of Alderworth House opened almost instantly after her maid rang the bell, a tall man ushering them into a room which was light and airy, the windows looking out on to a garden filled with greenery. A mismatched set of a sofa and two chairs were arranged before the fireplace and there were faded areas on the walls where pictures had been removed and never replaced. Lucinda wondered why the Duke had not had the place refurbished after his windfall in the Americas.

'I'll tell his Grace you are here, your Grace.' Ellesmere's butler's face flushed at the recognition of her name and he seemed to hesitate for a moment as if he could not quite decide what to do. 'It might take a few moments,' he managed finally. 'A maid will bring tea and cakes into you while you wait.'

'Thank you.'

Claire, her maid, stood by the door, her face a careful blank canvas. She was probably balancing the luxury of the Carisbrook houses against the frugality here, a topic that would be faithfully reported back to the downstairs staff at the Wellingham town house to mull over and discuss. Lucinda wished she might have asked her to wait with the carriage, but to do so would have invited questions.

She heard a cat howling outside somewhere close. Further afield the faint trip-trop of a carriage wending its way was audible above the ticking of an ancient ornate clock in the corner, its glass face shattered on one side and the time running a good half an hour slow.

The piece had already boomed out twice before the door opened again and Tay Ellesmere stood there, formally dressed and his gait stiff. His hair was wet, giving the impression he had just bathed, and it was pulled back into a tight tail falling to his shoulders. One eye was ringed in black whilst the white of the other had changed into a violent red, deeper marks of the same colour snaking into his hair at the temple. He smelled of soap and of lemon, a combination that was appealing, but all she could think of were Rosemary the scullery-maid's words: a small battered child lost behind hard green eyes.

'I am sorry. I did not realise we had arranged a meeting.'

'We had not, your Grace. It is just the last time I saw you it looked as though your injuries were worse than you let on and I thought to check to see if you were…well?'

'I am. Entirely.' The puffy edge of his right eye had made it close at one end. Lucinda wondered if it blurred his vision because he squinted as he watched her, the tick in his swollen eyelid clearly visible.

'I see.'

She wished with all her heart that they might have a moment in private. He seemed to understand her reticence as his glance took in the servants. 'Bingham, would you take the Duchess's maid to the kitchen and find her something to drink.'

'Very well, your Grace.' It took only a moment for the room to be cleared and the door to be shut behind them.

'A walk in the park would be out of the question, I suppose?' She kept her tone light as she broke the awkward silence.

'Unless you want me to scare small children.' His smile went nowhere near his eyes. 'Why are you here?' Tiredness draped the query.

'I have waited for you for the past two days and

when you did not come I wondered if you had the medical help that you needed…'

'I do.'

He did not even look at her now.

'What was the reason for your attack on Halsey all those years ago?'

That brought his attention back. 'Allenby broke one of the most important rules of my house.'

'Which was?'

'What goes on at Alderworth stays there.'

Disappointment welled. So it wasn't solely because he had been trying to protect her, after all.

'It seems to me enforcing such a rule would require much effort?' The sharpness in her voice was not becoming, but she could no longer hide it. 'Why seek more battles when you had enough of your own to fight?'

'Usually I am more handy with my fists than you saw me to be at the Chesterfields', and making certain scandal does not follow each of my guests home has not been unduly onerous before.'

Today Taylen Ellesmere was exactly the Duke his title proclaimed him to be, the solemn answers at odds with his damaged face and eyes. He stood strangely, too, straight-backed and erect, the pose making her wonder what other injuries he had sustained under the ministration of Halsey and his cronies.

'But scandal follows you regardless, your Grace. Your own reputation has been the talk of the town for years.'

He moved towards her and reached out his hand, one finger tracing its way down her cheek.

'Every opinion should be allowed to be given freely, I believe, but it is wise to remember that what is said is not always the truth.'

The warmth and the strength of him flooded into her being, a touchstone in the scattered uncertainty of her life, drawing her home.

Hold me closer, she longed to say, as if their history together melded only into the bright promise of this moment, but his hand fell back instead.

'If you don't wish to be in my company for a while, I would quite understand. I cannot promise that there will not be another contretemps, you see, and if you were to be hurt because of it...'

He stopped.

'I am no weak-willed girl, your Grace. Were I to be pitted against your own skills with a bow and arrow I may well win the competition.' She held her palms face up. 'I have the calluses to prove it.'

For the first time that day true humour crept into his face. 'My Diana.' The words were whispered and then regretted. She could see the wariness in his eyes.

'Do you have any other family at all, your Grace?'

His brow creased at the subject change.

'Why do you ask?'

'You seem so alone sometimes. I only wondered if there were others you might rely on.'

He shook his head and crossed to pour himself a

drink, lifting a brandy decanter to offer her one as well. Declining, she waited until he began to speak.

'I have an aunt, but I lost any contact with her years ago.'

'A fading line, then?'

His smile was wicked. 'Which brings us back to our agreement.'

The heir. With a thick cloak on, servants just outside the door and her maid presumably returning at any moment Lucinda also smiled. 'A broken nose and cracked ribs have probably put paid to any designs you might have on me at the moment.'

His laughter filled the room, deep and resonant. 'Injuries such as these have not stopped me before.'

'I read of you once. A story in a newspaper when you had first struck gold.'

'Where did you get it from?'

'An old school friend's brother sent it to me. The author of the piece made certain that the readers understood that the women you were partying with were...'' She could not quite find the word.

'Fallen?' He provided it for her. 'The difference between the *ton* and those who ply their bodies for money on the street corners of hopelessness is smaller than you might imagine. Believe me, I know it to be true.'

Was he speaking of his childhood? she wondered and braved a question. 'How did your uncle hurt you?'

'Badly.'

A truth, without an embroidered qualifying word attached? Lucinda could barely believe his honesty.

'He should have been shot.'

'He was.'

'Oh.'

The words were on her tongue to ask by whom, but the gleam in his green eyes stopped the question. She wanted amiability and agreement to be between them, even if only for this meeting.

'Would you ride with me tomorrow, your Grace? In the park. I usually go early before the crowds arrive.'

'Yes.'

She could hear the voices of her maid and one of the Ellesmere servants in the hallway coming closer. 'Shall we say nine o'clock?'

He reached over and rang the bell, the same man she had seen before hurrying back in. Claire also rejoined them, standing behind the sofa, a heavy frown upon her brow.

'Thank you for taking the time to see that I was regaining in strength, Duchess, and please do give my regards to your family.'

'I will, your Grace.'

So formal. So many undertones. She hoped with all her heart that her maid would say nothing of the visit to Asher's valet before she had had the chance to tell her brother.

'I went to see Taylen Ellesmere today,' Lucinda announced at dinner just as the main course was being served. On the journey home she had decided that honesty would be the best ploy with her family and bringing things out into the open was far better than having them simmer and boil over in the shadows.

'How is his face?' Emerald asked, her smile belying any more sinister purpose.

'I do not know if his nose is broken, though the boots of Halsey's minions did a good job of trying to do so. Both his eyes are blackened and there is a sizeable cut to the back of his head. Perhaps other injuries linger beneath his clothes. He certainly moved as if they did.'

'Trouble follows him like a stray dog after the meat man.' Her brother's voice was wary.

'I remember a time when it seemed to follow me with as much tenacity.' Emerald looked directly at Asher and the spark that ignited between them had Lucinda glancing away. Passion in a marriage bed was something she had never experienced, the burn of it rolling across ordinariness and lifting everything up. Every one of her siblings had that sort of feeling with their partner and she was suddenly tired of her own lack of hope for the same.

'I have asked the Duke to accompany me on my morning ride in the park tomorrow.'

'And he has agreed?' There was no warmth in her brother's query whatsoever. 'You may regret allowing a man who seems to find a fight at every oppor-

tunity, unprovoked or not, back into your life, Lucy.'
Fury raised the tone of his voice.

'He is my legal husband.'

'A matter that was supposed to be resolved three
years ago by a large sum of money. We hoped never
to see him again and we would not have, save for a
lucky strike in a Godforsaken goldfield miles from
England which allowed him to crawl back.'

Lucinda stood, breath coming almost as fast as
her heart was beating. 'Perhaps that is divine inter-
vention, then. Gold for gold and the recommencing
of an ordained union promised before a minister of
the Church. Surely when you hatched this plan of
matrimony a small part of you thought that it might
just…stick?'

Asher stood now, too, and Lucinda was glad that
the table lay between them, a solid wide slab of oak
that divided the room down its length.

'God damn it, you are my sister and I was only
trying to protect you.' For the first time in memory
her oldest brother sounded…defeated, the strain of
the last week showing on his face in deep lines of
regret.

'And you do that well, but I do not wish to live
with you for ever. I need to find my own life, too.'

'I will gift you Amberley Manor in Kent, then.
That estate is more than ample for your needs. You
can stay there with a stipend if you cannot stay here.'

'But I will still be beholden to your generosity,
don't you see, and with no recourse to marriage again

it will always be that way. For ever. Until I am old and childless and alone.'

'So you would agree instead to give the benefit of doubt to a Duke who displays neither morality nor virtue? A man you hate?'

'Eleanor seems to think he is more virtuous than any of us might realise, Asher.' Emerald came around the table to stand by Lucinda, her turquoise eyes deep pools of worry. 'She says that the servants at his London town house have a great deal of regard for him.'

'You imagine that is enough?'

'Cristo said Alderworth dealt with Halsey when he was spreading rumours of Lucinda's...dalliance. He seems to believe Halsey waylaid him to pay him back. If that is the case, we ought to be thanking him, not maligning him.' She stopped for a moment before carrying on. 'It is also rumoured that Alderworth still supports the wife and children of his mining partner, killed in an accident in America. Only an honourable person would do that.'

Unexpectedly her brother began to laugh. 'Lord, Emmie, if we want to find out about anyone it would be wise to ask you first.'

'All I am saying is that he may be a good man whom you have not given a chance to.'

'A good man who locked my sister in a room against her will and had her way with her. That sort of a good man?'

'Well, if Lucy finds that she cannot bear him, then

she can take you up on your offer of Amberley. It is not medieval England after all. Alderworth cannot keep her anywhere against her will.'

The thought that he might do just that showed on Asher's face as a dark uncertainty, but the heart of his argument had been taken to pieces and Lucinda knew that Asher would allow her the freedom she asked for. However, when she exchanged a smile of gratitude with her sister-in-law, she saw in the turquoise eyes a quick burst of puzzlement and pity before she turned for the door.

Chapter Ten

❧❧❧

As Lucinda brushed away a curl that had escaped her bonnet in the wind, a movement to one side of the park caught her eye.

Taylen Ellesmere watched her from a distance and she waited as he threaded his way towards her on a large dark stallion.

'You ride well,' he said as he reached her. Today his bruising looked less and he moved with more ease, though his right eye was still brutally red.

'You have been watching me?'

'I had heard you had a good seat.' His left hand shifted on the reins and the rings on his fingers caught in the sun, underlining the differences between them. Such adornment seemed an over-embellishment and foreign, though she was pleased to see that the ring she had given him as a wedding vow still lay amongst the others. He hailed from a world that was so far removed from her own that Lucinda wondered if she might ever truly know him.

When he saw where she looked he stilled, the vigilance that seldom left his eyes easily seen.

'I ride here most days when I am in town, your Grace. It is a freeing thing.'

'I have also heard it said that you tool a barouche like a champion.'

She laughed. 'Taris taught me.'

'You are fortunate, then, in the care your family gives you.'

She wished her brothers had heard the compliment he gave them, for perhaps then they might not have been quite so averse to any communication. The breeze caught at a line of oaks to one side of the path, sending a scattering of green leaves into the air.

'I think the early morning shows Hyde Park at its best,' she chanced when he did not deign to speak.

'Indeed. My grandfather loved it here, too. It was the closest he ever got to a peaceful and solitary life given my grandmother's disposition, for he spent all of his hours wandering the parks and gardens when he was in town.'

'He sounds kind.'

'He was.'

'How old were you when he died?'

'Six and a half.' So precisely known, Lucinda thought.

'I met Lady Shields a few times. She seemed difficult.'

'And now she lies beside my grandfather in consecrated ground for all of eternity.'

'Matrimony being the most onerous of bonds to break away from?' The sting in her voice did not become her, but his last words made her wonder if that was what he might think of their union, too.

He was quiet for a moment. 'There are things about marriage that one could find…addictive.'

She thought he meant sex and stiffened, but when he kept on talking she knew that that was not what he was alluding to at all.

'A person to watch your back and be on your side no matter what happens is one of them. I do not think I thanked you enough for doing just that the other night at the Chesterfields' Ball. No one ever has before.'

Again she saw behind the mask, a quick glimpse of a man she could love. A lot.

'I was glad to help.' So precise and stilted. She wished he would dismount and reach out to thank her with his body, but he did not, his attention caught by others riding behind them.

Shifting in his seat, his horse shied to one side and he gentled him. A few other souls had now ventured out on the same pathways, tipping their hats as they passed and looking back with more than interest on their faces. Tay knew the gossip mills had been grinding ever since his return to England and that the betting in the clubs were riding fifty to one he would have his estranged wife beneath him before the week's end.

He might have enjoyed the irony of it all, but such a gamble cut too close to the quick and fifty to one still seemed like damn long odds. He hoped that the Wellingham brothers had no knowledge of the punters' flutterings.

The stakes were rising and he could not get Lucinda to himself until at least after the promised two weeks.

Breathing deeply, he bid his horse on and was glad when his wife followed his lead, the path wider now and more conducive to a canter. There was nothing like a ride to free a soul of tension and the heavy muscles beneath him were soothing and easeful.

Lucinda rode like the youngest sister of three brothers who had all left the mark of their tutorship upon her, fluid and daring, and he allowed her by him so that he might watch. She did not flaunt her gift, but every movement and command had the sort of controlled gentleness that even great horsemen struggled to achieve as she galloped in front of him. Her laughter rang in the air as she pulled in her mount, waiting as he drew up beside her.

'I don't know of another female who can ride with the expertise of a jockey.'

'You disapprove?'

'Far from it, my lady wife. I hail it. At Alderworth you will find fine tracks to ride along, though the stables have been largely depleted.'

'But you will replace them with new stock?'

He shook his head. 'To get the production from the land up and running again is my first priority.'

'You do not sound as dissolute as they say, then.'

'It is my experience that no one is ever as good or as bad as society might paint them.'

A slight flush crawled into her cheeks. 'Expectations are certainly bonds that tie you down. The Wellingham name held me captive for years in that I could never truly be myself.'

'And now?'

'When everybody disapproves so firmly of my actions, it gives a freedom to do just as I want.'

There it was again, that sadness. The accident, a hasty marriage and his three years away had all had their part in drawing a melancholy hue over her pale-blue eyes. Ever since they had met they had hurt each other, Tay thought, his demands for an heir adding to the burden. He was suddenly tired of it.

'Lucinda. Luce.' A sound from a distance had them both turning. A young woman hailed them from her mare, her groom left far behind.

'My friend, Posy Tompkins. You will remember her from the wedding.'

'She was the one who brought you to Alderworth in the first place?'

When she nodded Tay thought he had a lot to thank Miss Tompkins for. He watched as she came closer.

* * *

Lucinda wished that they had ridden further into the greenery where they might have been more alone to talk. Already she could see the intrigue on her friend's face.

'I have been following you,' Posy said as she joined them, 'and I still think you should not take such risks on a horse, Lucy. How many times have your brothers admonished you not to gallop so fast?'

'Oh, I lost count months ago.'

'The doctor told you another bump on the head could be dangerous…'

'He did?' Taylen Ellesmere sounded nothing like he had a few moments prior. Nay, now he sounded exactly the same as Cristo, Asher and Taris.

Posy nodded. 'He said that she was to lead a careful and circumspect life and that he had seen many a patient becoming gravely ill if they did not heed his advice.'

The green in her husband's eyes displayed no humour now whatsoever.

'Something about blood vessels bursting, I think he said. The walls of the brain are thinner where they have been damaged. Because of that it is easier for them to erupt again.' Listing the medical information using her fingers, she bent down each one after every fact stated.

Posy did not look at her, but at Alderworth, an expression that Lucinda recognised on her face. The same look she had seen in their earlier days when together they would stage outlandish tragedies for the family to watch, the curtains in the downstairs salon of Falder fashioned into a theatre. She was baiting Alderworth for some reason and Lucinda could do nothing at all to stop it.

'Posy is exaggerating and I hardly think that will happen, your Grace—' she began, but Taylen interrupted her.

'Are you a physician now, too?' The tone in his voice was furious.

'No.'

'Then you should heed a warning from a man who is obviously qualified to give it.'

'And never race along the gullies and cliffs at Falder? Never clear another fence in my life?'

'If that is what it takes to be safe from any danger, then yes.'

Posy's laughter brought an end to the bickering. 'Asher has used the same arguments as you do so many times, your Grace, but to no avail.' Posy raised her eyebrows as Lucinda frowned at her and smiled congenially at Alderworth.

Amazing, Lucinda thought. Posy had never approved of any of her suitors. Not one. It was the creases in Taylen Ellesmere's cheeks, she supposed, and the way the light played upon his eyes—a man who was no one's lackey. The only white he wore was in his cravat and it showed up the tan of his skin. She could suddenly imagine him far from London in the back country wilds of Georgia, traipsing across swollen rivers and steep craggy mountains. Any information she had ever read on goldfields described them as hard and dangerous places, spawning hard and dangerous men.

'My brothers have this idea that I need to be looked after all the time. I find it easier to simply get on with my life in the way that I wish to and allow them to do the same.'

'In other words, you do not tell them of the danger you are placing yourself in.'

'Exactly, and I would appreciate your discretion in the matter, too, your Grace.'

'Then I hope you will at least have the sense to walk your horse home.' He tipped his hat. 'Miss Tompkins, it was my pleasure.'

Then he was gone, cutting across the park on a path Lucinda seldom used, body rising and falling with each movement of his horse in an effortless display of skill.

'Alderworth rides well, Luce.'

Anger seeped into her reply. 'Why would that be important to me, Posy? If it was left to everyone else, I should be in my drawing room at home, pursuing the gentle arts of needlework or playing music.'

Or lying in bed on my back, trying to produce an Ellesmere heir.

She bit down on chagrin.

'What the hell are you doing here, Alderworth?'

'White's is my club too, Wellingham, and I want a chat with you.'

Cristo Wellingham did not assent, but neither did he get up and leave. Rather he sat with his drink in hand and waited until Tay had taken the chair opposite.

'Your sister is recklessly galloping in Hyde Park when, according to a Miss Posy Tompkins, her doctor has expressly discouraged such behaviour.'

The other took a large swallow of his brandy before putting it down. 'And now you want to stop her?'

'I do.'

'Well, good luck with that. Asher's response was to take her horses away for a month, but she only hired other more dangerous ones. Taris endeavoured to send a man with her every time she used the stables, but she gave him the slip more times than not. I took her to Graveson where she rode along the beaches until she got bored with them. A number of approaches, you see, and none of them worked well or for long because she is as stubborn as a mule and twice as difficult.'

'A true Wellingham, then?'

Cristo tipped back his head and laughed. 'If you were not such a bastard, Alderworth, I might even like you. What is in it for you, anyway, this sudden and touching concern for my sister?'

'I do not wish to be a widower.'

Again Cristo laughed. 'You have not as yet been a husband and, if my family has its way, you never will be.'

Ignoring the criticism, Tay went straight to the heart of the matter. 'What else interests her?'

Cristo leant forwards, a frown on his face. 'She enjoys archery. No danger and a quiet walk to the target. She is also inclined to drawing. But be warned that if you play false with her emotions this time, Alderworth, there won't be any second chances.'

'Word has it that you got one with your wife.'

'Word has it you were in gaol in the Americas for taking the life of another.'

'Gold makes bad men greedy and rumour is always overstated.'

'As greedy as you were when you hived off with the Wellingham booty after despoiling our sister?' The quiet of Cristo Wellingham's words belied the fury inside each one.

'You know as well as I that I have paid every pound of it back and Lucinda was an innocent when I left her, no matter what she remembers.'

'Edmund Coleridge may have changed that, of course.'

Tay's fist came down on the table. 'If I hear even the slightest of whispers from him saying anything of the sort, then he will be a dead man.'

'I will tell him when I see him next. He is a personal friend of mine.'

'You do just that.'

Swallowing the last of his brandy, Taylen stood, the peers of the realm of England watching him over their tipples. The Alderworth ducal title sat squarely on him, but he had never felt that he belonged here, the stuffy manners and pretensions of these men so far from his own road in life.

He wanted to get back to Alderworth and he wanted to take his wife with him. The face of Edmund Coleridge rose into his consciousness and he stalked from the room.

Coleridge was kissing Lucinda's hand when Tay met her next at an afternoon soirée at the house of Daniel and Camille Beauchamp.

His wife had not frequented the pathways of Hyde Park that morning to take her exercise. He had been waiting, after all, but as the minutes had turned to hours he knew she would not come.

He was therefore both relieved to find her here and furious to see who she was with, for the man was virtually making love to her with his lips and she was allowing it. Her compliancy had him grating his teeth together. Hard.

'Duchess.'

She frowned and he was pleased to see worry in her eyes. 'Duke.'

Coleridge made no attempt at all to distance himself from her side and Taylen looked at him pointedly as his wife began to speak.

'Cristo said you might want to talk to me.' The statement left Tay speechless. 'He said you had a proposition you would like me to know. Something about spending my days in the parlour with my embroidery or being coddled in the garden painting flowers?'

'Your youngest brother has a sense of humour.'

'You went to see him after our meeting in the park? You went to tell him about my galloping when I so expressly asked you not to?'

Coleridge was taking in every word between them with interest and Tay had had enough. 'Would you excuse us?' Without waiting for a reply he shepherded his wife to an end of the room sheltered from the notice of others by a narrow alcove.

'I did not expect you to be so…underhanded,' Lucinda said as they stopped, her eyes shimmering with anger. Taylen changed tack altogether.

'I told your brother I did not fancy living alone for the rest of my life if anything were to happen to you. Did he tell you that as well?'

She shook her head.

'Edmund Coleridge wants you in his bed.'

'A fact that makes him little different from you then, your Grace.'

He ignored her criticism completely. 'Yet knowing that, you still allow him to court you openly?'

'He is a friend. I allow him friendship.'

'Your brother thinks he would like to be very much more.'

'It sounds like you had a long discussion about me. Pity I was not there to set wrongs to right, but then my siblings have always been more than quick to make judgements about the suitability of my various beaux.'

'Various?'

'Indeed. You didn't expect me to be pining for the company of a husband who did not think to remember that he had a wife for three long years until the necessity for a legitimate heir brought him back?'

The four small stars on her bracelet sparked gold as her hands underlined her words.

'The newspaper cutting you spoke of, the one in the paper from Georgia. It was not as it was reported. Since marrying you I have always respected my vows and I have not…cheated.' He finished each word with a sharp honesty. The muscles in his jaw rippled with the effort.

Damn, Taylen thought, what the hell had made him confess that to his estranged wife here in a crowded room in the middle of a public soirée?

He was known for his waywardness and his belief in free speech and action, flamboyant and untempered by the conventions attached to society life. He had lived his whole life in the pursuit of the hedonistic and the liberal, escaping the dreadfulness of his childhood with fine wine and finer women.

Until he had married!

Then something had happened that he could not explain. His libido, long since more than active, had simply dried up and he found it difficult to touch a woman without thinking of his parents' licentiousness. Six lovers had trooped through his younger life

on his mother's side and many, many more than that
on his father's. And they had left their mark.

He remembered the chaos as if it were yesterday
and had vowed every moment of his early years never
to repeat it if and when he finally married.

His hands tightened at his sides, fisting into hardness. It was why he had returned to England, after
all, to understand just exactly what it was that simmered between him and this woman he had been
forced into a union with.

Lucinda, the only wife he was ever likely to have
and to hold. If it had not all been so deadly serious
he would have laughed at his conundrum. A sinner
caught by a saint and made impotent to boot by the
memory of his parents' unfaithfulness.

Nothing made sense any more and had not done
so for a long time. He wanted his certainty back and
his conviction and one small part of him understood
that only with Lucinda at his side might he be able
to regain it.

It was the reason he had pressed her so hard with
his need for an heir—a way to bring her to him on
his own terms. A way to bed her.

Lucinda could not believe what she had just heard.
The Dissolute Duke of Alderworth was telling her
he had been faithful to her memory? All those years.
All those temptations. Three thousand miles from
home and a stranger in a land that was as harsh as it
was different and yet he had never cheated? A Duke

who was known for his dalliances and excesses? She was astonished.

'Why are you telling me this?'

'Because I want to know that any child we do have is actually mine.'

The anger in his voice contradicted everything he was confessing. One moment she understood him and the next…

'I was brought up with a father who never believed that I was his, you see, and treated me accordingly. Seeing what such distrust does to a man, I should not like to repeat it.' No softness lay in his brittle green eyes, the bruising around them adding to his menace. 'It is not necessary that you like me when you provide me with an heir, Duchess, but I do need to be certain that you have not allowed another the same delights.'

My goodness, she could barely breathe with her anger and confusion, the joy of the disclosure eradicated completely by a reading of her character that was hardly salubrious.

He imagined *her* wanton? The pulse in her throat was beating like a drum as she stood speechless. At that moment she hated him with a passion and she could not keep the emotion from showing on her face.

'I shall be leaving London for Alderworth on the morrow. I will send the carriage back for you when I have word that you wish to join me.'

He was disappearing again, the tenuous truce that

she had felt between them across the last week dissolving. Even in the face of her fury she could not just watch him go.

'What time will you leave?' Her voice sounded broken and hoarse.

'In the morning. There is no point in staying here longer.'

'Then I will come, too.'

For the first time a spark of life entered his eyes. 'Very well. My carriage will be at the Wellingham town house at ten o'clock. Be ready.'

He did not speak again before he turned and walked away, Edmund Coleridge joining her the moment he was gone.

'You look pale. If Ellesmere has threatened you—?'

'No.' She did not let him finish. As a friend of Cristo's she realised he might know more of the relationship she had with Alderworth than others did. 'I think I am just tired.'

Taking a breath, she tried to regain her lost composure, all the while her eyes scouting to check if Taylen Ellesmere was still anywhere in the vicinity.

'I am retiring to Bath next week with my family, Lucy. If you should wish to join us, you would be more than welcome. My mother would enjoy having you to stay, I am sure.'

Edmund's eyes were warm with promise, but Lucinda knew she could no longer lead him on with hopes that would never come to pass.

'I am sorry. I shall be rejoining my husband at Alderworth tomorrow. It has just been decided.'

'I see.' He stepped back. 'Does Cristo know what you intend?'

'Not yet, but he will.'

'He won't be pleased.'

Ignoring his condemnation, she carried on. 'I wish you well in your Bath sojourn. I imagine it is lovely there at this time of the year.'

Platitudes, she knew, but her husband's unexpected confession had taken her from one place to another.

Taylen Ellesmere had never cheated on her, but had held their marriage vows safe and close. She felt the smile blossom on her face as she gave Coleridge her goodbyes and went to find Camille Beauchamp to thank her for the soirée.

Chapter Eleven

'I would feel far happier about all of this if you would take a few of the Wellingham servants with you.'

Lucinda shook her head at Taris's words. She did not want those in the employ of her brothers to see the truth of the relationship she had with Taylen Ellesmere, for undoubtedly such a detail would leak back to Falder. She was pleased when the conversation was interrupted.

'The Alderworth conveyance is here, my lord.'

'Very well. See that Lady Lucinda's luggage is stowed on board.'

Taris turned to her as the butler left. 'Asher and Emerald have decided not to see you off and Eleanor and Cristo were called back to Graveson yesterday afternoon. Perhaps it is best that it is just us.'

When her middle brother stood she went into his embrace, his arms warm around her, the solid strength and honesty of him so very familiar. Part of her wanted to hold on and stay here, under the shelter of home and family, but another part needed something different and that was the voice she was heeding.

Disengaging her arms, she moved away, trying to keep her emotions in check.

'I shall send word as soon as I am there to let you know that I am safe.'

'It is not the journey worrying me, Lucy, but the man who you will live with at destination's end.'

The amber in his eyes was clouded and she could see worry there. It broke her heart to sense her brother's concern. Just another betrayal she had heaped upon the family. Beatrice, however, was smiling.

'Go with hope, Lucinda, and find the way of your life.' She pressed a small package into her hand. 'I have wrapped up a book for you I have recently enjoyed.'

And then Lucinda was outside, the façade of the town house behind her in the wind. Looking up at the third-floor window, she fancied she saw Asher, but the shadow was gone before she had time to be certain.

One step, two steps and then three, her feet like leaden weights dragging towards the carriage. Taylen Ellesmere sat inside and gave Taris a cursory greeting which was given back with an equal lack of warmth. When the door was closed between them, her brother's open palm splayed out upon the window.

I love you. She mouthed the words, but knew that he would not see them. Biting down on the soft flesh inside her bottom lip, she sat back as the horses gathered their rhythm.

'I am not taking you away for ever, Lucinda. You may return any time you wish to visit your family. The carriage shall be at your disposal whenever you have need of it.'

She nodded because she did not trust herself to speak and he swore beneath his breath.

'My own family was not close so it is something of a novelty to see such affection in others,' he offered finally as she kept her silence. 'In fact, I would say loathing was the nearest term to describe any family dynamics that I recall.'

'That must have been difficult for you.'

'Well, it was always easier when distance parted us.' He smiled through the gloom of the day, a laconic devil-may-take-it smile that negated all that she had ever heard of his upbringing. 'I would be farmed out to others, with no thought given to my schooling. My life truly began when I eventually got to Eton.'

A new and interesting turn. 'How old were you?'

'Twelve. My parents had died the year before, but I was an independent child for my age so their deaths barely affected me.'

'Callous.'

'I prefer to call it practical.'

A dead end of insults slung across lies.

'One of the maids at Falder used to work for your grandmother at about the same time you did not return from France.'

He stiffened and Lucinda felt a creeping coldness. A muscle along the bottom of his jaw ground out movement when she chanced a peek at him.

'Rosemary Jones made some mention of your uncle.'

This time he sat forwards, his hands together so that his fingers were entwined in the position Lucinda remembered placing her own in one of the favoured games of childhood.

Here is the church and here is the steeple...

Ditties that he would not have played as he was fighting for his life in a hospital bed in Rouen.

'She said that you were often hurt.' This was blurted out before she lost her courage altogether.

'All children need to stand corrected in the name of good behaviour.'

His eyes flinted, the anger in them causing her to simply fold. She could have said more, could have told him everything that the maid had confided, but it was too soon and the facts were too raw.

'Of course they do, your Grace.' She sounded like a thousand other wives in London who only wanted a life that was peaceful and easy, the truth tearing what contentment was left into pieces.

Outside the road ran along fields of green and the sky was blue, a cold blue, the colour belying the temperature. It was chilly inside the carriage, too, and she was pleased for the woollen blanket that was over her lap.

She wondered where the accident in the carriage had occurred when they had come this way all those years ago. She had been told the name of the place, of course, but with no little memory left of the time, she could be certain of nothing. Still she felt a familiarity, a knowledge of having passed this way before and she was glad that the journey would be only a few hours in length.

Taylen Ellesmere had ceased to make any effort at conversation at all, his glance drawn by the views outside, his face a blank mask of indifference. If he remembered the accident, he did not show it.

Over the past week she thought she might have been getting closer to him, but this morning they sat opposite each other like strangers hurtling towards a new life together and one it seemed that neither of them wanted. When her fingers closed around the jade talisman of happiness that Emerald had bequeathed her, she frowned.

She wished she might ask him to explain more of his surprising confession from yesterday and that this time instead of anger there could be dialogue. But his expression stopped her from such an action and so she turned to look out at the countryside.

Alderworth was a substantial mansion built of stone and wood, the wings around a large central edifice a matching image of each other. The parkland it sat in was extensive, rows of old trees stretching as far as the eye could see. A lake of some proportion lay at the bottom of a rise, the old stone walls radiating out from the driveway alluding to another, more ancient dwelling.

Lucinda had come last time under the cover of darkness. She knew because Posy had filled in many of the details of the visit that she had forgotten. She hoped that the servants would not remember her and that enough time had passed for the incident to be consigned to history and to never be recalled.

'When my parents were alive they used to line the servants up around the front driveway every time a guest came to stay in a sort of skewed sense of importance. I have never been so formal.'

'It looks…' She could not quite voice what she meant to say.

'Less than well cared for?' His eyes took in the lines of the house. 'Much of the money at the moment is going into increasing the production of the agricultural yields.'

'Cristo has been doing the same at Graveson.'

'Then perhaps we have more in common than I thought.'

'So there are no more parties here?'

He turned towards her and Lucinda felt breathless. 'The shallow follies of youth have much to be accountable for. I spend money on far more important things now.'

Like the production of an heir?

She almost said it. Almost blurted it out, so that it was there in the open instead of seething underneath each and every word, a contract penned in pragmatism and shame. Instead she smiled, in a tight and vapid way, the movement taking the humour from his eyes.

'You will have your own set of rooms and a maid to see to your needs. The house has suffered across the years from inattention but I am aiming to see it restored.'

'You love Alderworth, then?'

'History is to be valued,' he answered in a measured way. 'If too much of it is left to waste, there will be no lessons to be learnt by those who come after us.'

The topic of the heir again, winding into conversation and strangling any hope of accord. Best to remember that she was not here as the cherished new wife of a Duke who would love her, but as the sole hope of ensuring that a questionable family name might march into yet another decade of unbroken lineage.

When the carriage stopped and Lucinda was helped out by a servant who welcomed her, she was achingly aware that Taylen Ellesmere neither took her arm nor gave her the courtesy of any introduction as they walked inside.

Not quite the wife he wanted, but at least the country air made her feel stronger and more in control.

Everything here was in need of attention: the flaky stone, the gardens, the few servants in their old and faded uniforms. Ellesmere had not lied when he had proclaimed the finances of Alderworth had suffered.

But beneath the lack of care, peeling paint and rotten woodwork was a beauty that lay in the very bones of the place, the house's roofline raised to the sky in a proud exclamation of old wealth.

The quality of the timber was undeniable, the ornate cornices alluding to a time where such frippery was the vogue. She vaguely remembered parts of it from the last time she had been here and did her best to recollect more, but to no avail. Darkly fashioned paintings of ancestors stared down from the walls in every room, sombre harsh people whose eyes seemed to follow this new generation with a disapproval that was tangible.

Two large portraits of his parents had pride of place above the fire surround in the main salon and Lucinda saw the small holes a dart might fashion in both of them before she had looked away, not wishing to pry further. A green *chaise-longue* with carved mahogany feet took up the space in a bay window, the sun lightening the fabric in all the places that it had touched, leaving the seams dark.

Taylen Ellesmere had disappeared almost immediately, leaving her in the hands of a middle-aged housekeeper, Mrs Berwick, who had hurried her up to the first floor and finally to her bedchamber, a room nearly at the very end of a long corridor. She had pointed out a pile of bath cloths and two decanters with brandy and whisky, equally filled on a table by the bedside.

An evening tipple? The single glass provided looked spotlessly clean.

'There is a light meal set out for your lunch in the small dining room, your Grace, and dinner will be served at six. When you require a maid to help you dress you only have to ring the bell and she will come.'

The bed was tiny, a child's cot that gladdened her heart, for there was no possible way her large husband could share it with her.

After the accompanying luggage was lifted into place she thanked the two men with a smile. Around the edge of the room stood many tallboys and wardrobes, the array of old furniture giving the impression that many of the unwanted accoutrements of the Ellesmere lineage had been dumped here, a last resting place before being disposed of or burnt.

When the woman didn't leave, Lucinda knew there was something important that she wished to impart to her. 'The master has brought new life to Alderworth, your Grace. The house may not be as magnificent as it once was, but the farm cottages have been refurbished and the people here appreciate his endeavours. He is a good man despite all that might be said of him in London.'

The woman hurried out after she had delivered her words, a swish of skirt and then gone.

A good master who was appreciated here? Lucinda turned the words on her tongue, liking the endorsement.

Nerves had taken away hunger, so she walked to the window to gaze down upon the gardens, the formal lines of hedges lost in the march of time. No one had tended to anything, it seemed, the wild and rambling roses climbing in a tangled heap of runners with the occasional misshaped flower blooming amidst green. The hand of good fortune had disappeared a long time ago from the estate of Alderworth, leaving disorder in its place. Her mind dwelled on the fact that her husband was a Duke who would make sure others were well housed before he turned his attention to his own living quarters and she smiled.

A movement caught her eye in the very far corner of her view. Ellesmere was hurrying towards the stable courtyard a little way off, his demeanour brisk. He had dispensed with his jacket and his hat and the white linen of his shirt stretched across the muscles of his back, his dark hair trailing across it. Another came out to meet him, a small round man waving his arms madly as if in some important explanation. The Duke in contrast stood perfectly still, a quiet centre in the midst of all that moved about him.

Taylen Ellesmere did that often, she thought, as though testing the air, like a deer might in the high hills of some undisturbed place just to make certain of safety.

Then a horse came forth, a stallion of a height Lucinda had not seen before, the lines of Arabia in its form. She saw her husband run his hands across its flanks, quiet and gentle, before he mounted, easily managing the skittish response of the animal. The Duke of Alderworth looked as though he had been born there, the flow of man and beast joined in a languid and perfect balance as he turned towards the hills beyond the gardens and disappeared.

Then there was nothing, only trees and leaves and the scudding clouds across the afternoon sky wending towards a dark forest in the distance.

She wished she could open the doors that led out on to a balcony to see if she might catch more of a glimpse of them, but they were nailed shut—another oddity in a house full of neglect. Lifting her hand, she wrote her initials on the inside of the window. With a flourish she surrounded her name with the shape of a heart and then rubbed the whole thing out, her fingers made dirty by the dust on the glass.

Falder, her family home, had the lines of love running through it, generations of Wellinghams enjoying the promise. Each day a legion of staff cleaned it from top to toe until it was polished and gleaming, the small decay of everyday living repaired before any damage had the chance to spread further.

The sun broke out quite suddenly, enhancing the green in the fields behind. Here in the rolling hills of

Bedfordshire and far from the expectations of London there was a certain peace and freedom she had not felt in years. It lay, she supposed, in the march of time drawn across a fading splendour. Once Alderworth would have boasted grandeur and sumptuousness, but there was a mellow truth about its present-day meagreness that was beguiling.

Finding her satchel, she drew forth her drawing equipment and laid a parchment on the desk, liking the feel of charcoal, the dusty ease of a long-time friend calming in the face of the unknown. She drew, from memory, the house and its lines and Taylen Ellesmere on the horse, his hair against the wind, his forehead strong.

She stopped after sketching his eyes and rested because the quickness in them was disconcerting, knowing, a question framed in them that held all her own fears naked in the afternoon light. She wanted to rub them out, wanted to scrawl across such eyes with a hard strong stroke, but she couldn't. Couldn't countenance destruction of such raw and angry beauty. His lips followed, full and generous, lips that had offered her the promise of liberty for the price of a child. Yet he had qualified such an unexpected option with salvation and loyalty and she believed he had meant it.

Placing one finger across the drawing, she felt an easing of spirit, a lessening of tightness. A slight question of flesh? Revealing. Unforeseen.

'Taylen.' She whispered the name into the quiet

and even as she watched his lips seemed to turn. Upwards. The black of charcoal moving in a way it never had before. Living. Breathing. Laughing. She did not dare to impart more form to his figure as she buried the sheet of paper in her sketchbook.

A flash of some hidden thing ripped through Lucinda, beating at truth. The headaches she had had after the accident had largely gone, yet here they threatened to return in the same intensity as they had whilst convalescing.

A room came through the fog, a room at the end of a long corridor and a man sitting in bed and reading.

Spectacles. She had the vague idea it was Alderworth. She squinted her eyes to try to remember the title of the book in his hands because she thought it was important in some way. But no more memory surfaced.

Rising, she picked up her cloth bag from the place she had left it in one corner and extracted the wrapped present that Beatrice had bequeathed her in the moments before her departure from London. A novel confronted her as she ripped off the bright blue paper and a note was threaded with ribbon around the cover.

Lucy,
The dependence of women on marriage to secure social standing and economic security can be underpinned with something far more wonderful. I have a suspicion that you will find

what I allude to with Taylen Ellesmere. Anne
Elliot certainly did in this story.
All my love,
Bea

Jane Austen's *Persuasion*. She had not read this
book and was glad for the chance to do so here,
though Beatrice's note seemed more than odd. She
knew her brothers hated her husband with a passion and had thought her sister-in-law might have
felt the same.

Something wonderful? Such hollow hope was
layered with a reality far from any such truth, the
unfamiliar environment here increasing her homesickness.

When tears welled up behind her eyes she did not
try to stop them as they ran down her cheeks and on
to the small book across her lap, blurring the inked
note in Beatrice's handwriting.

Taylen waded naked into the lake behind the
house and waited as the icy water numbed his feet
and his legs, the shadow of Valkyrie reflected in the
silver before him, low in the water. He had named
this dash of raised-up land as a boy and had used
the island as a fortress many times, a stronghold
against a coercive uncle and a place to assuage the
remnants of betrayal.

'Betrayal.' He whispered the word to himself and
watched how the warm air fogged. He had never

had a chance against his mother's brother with his corrupt tastes and easy smile. The fact that he was a child whose parents saw responsibility only as a nuisance and had gladly given up any claim on a son who was alternatively badly behaved or withdrawn aided such tendencies.

Innocence was such an easily taken commodity and Taylen knew that his had gone a long time ago.

Like the small hut he had built on the rise, left to the birds and the ghosts and the wind. Only echoes in the inlets and silence in the few remaining trees, the black outline of wood sharp against the dusk where it had fallen at an angle against the sky. No longer a shelter.

Picking up a handful of sand, he let it filter through his fingers—Alderworth soil, the mark of a thousand years of ancestry imprinted in the earth. His land now, to have and to hold as certainly as a wife brought from London under the dubious flag of obligation.

He shook his head hard, the strands of wetness falling into his line of vision before he wiped them away. The air here strengthened him and gave him resolve. Lucinda would be sitting in the room beside his and wondering what exactly might happen next. He hated the fact that she would be frightened, but there was no other way of resolving this impasse, and he knew without a single doubt that had he left her in London her brothers would have made certain any access was limited.

Lord, but was it any better here? The whole place teetered under a strange spell of melancholy, the staff left reduced to a bare handful of overworked servants.

He had left it too long to return, he supposed, but the memories here had always repelled him, the child without rights struggling inside the man he had become, dissolute and uncaring. Swallowing, he fisted his hands hard against his thighs and lifted his face to the rain that had begun to fall in a mist.

Back. Again. This time with a spouse who distrusted him and the threat of retribution from the Wellinghams should he ever hurt her.

A flash of lightning above the hills to the east reflected in the lake. A sign, perhaps. A portent of battle.

That evening Lucinda came down the wide staircase with a feeling of disbelief, her heart tight and her stomach filled with butterflies. The dress she wore was her newest, light-yellow silk shot through with gold, the *décolletage* on the prim side of fashionable heightened by a line of frothy Brussels lace, her arms covered by a shawl against the cold. Her hair was pinned to her head in a tall and elegant chignon, with a few curls left to frame her face, that had taken a maid a good hour to complete. On her feet were slippers of fine calf leather, the lacings drawn in tight.

The Alderworth servant accompanying her

stepped back as they came into the front salon. In the ensuing silence a bead of sweat traced its way between her breasts to fall across the skin above her ribs.

Taylen Ellesmere was already there, dressed entirely in black, the collar at his neck open. A gentleman at home and at leisure or a man expecting a woman to entertain him?

'Duchess.' His teeth were white and even and perfect.

Part of her wanted to run, wanted to lift the embroidered fall of silk and make for the safety of her room, negating any contract between them.

I do not think he would stop me if I went! The thought came from nowhere but it was there in his eyes, soft velvet with a sort of pity.

She did not wish for that. Raising her chin, she walked through the opened door and tried not to flinch as it shut behind her.

His eyes took in her gown and her hair, his expression tightening. 'I have something to show you,' he said as the silence lengthened. 'It is this way.'

He did not take her hand or shepherd her forwards. He did not touch her at all, but walked in front through the long corridors of the place to a room filled with books. Two glasses sat on a desk with a bottle of white wine chilled in a bucket of ice.

Intentions, she supposed, a heady amount of alcohol to loosen the restraints of almost thirty-six months of distance.

'Please, take a seat.'

She chose a chair with enough room for one person. Unexpectedly, though, he pulled a stool over to where she was and sat in front of her. A shaft of light bathed him, turning his hair to shining raven black. Like the cut sides of coal. He was the most handsome man she had ever met. She could not dispute that fact.

'I was not intimate with you three years ago no matter what you might say, Lucinda. I put you in the carriage before anything could happen between us and tried to take you home. If it had not been for the accident, I would probably have succeeded.'

Lucinda felt her insides curl. Taylen Ellesmere had always used words well to suit his intentions.

'You were in bed. I remember you…touching me?'

'You ran into my room to escape from the Earl of Halsey. I kissed you once. That was all.'

'No.' She shook her head. 'You lie.' Her eyes flicked to the line of her breast though she could not bring herself to voice all that she remembered.

His fingers at her nipples, the feel of him hard against her skin in places no one had ever touched before. The full naked size of him as he stood before her. Shocking. Thrilling. Forbidden.

Reaching over to the wine, he poured her a glass, fine crystal, and the stem vibrated under the pressure of her fingers as she took it. As easy to break as her innocence had been?

'Perhaps a drink might refresh your tangled memory,' he toasted, shattering the bubble of *détente* completely. A sharp bud of shock took her breath as hard eyes gleamed, the warmth of his glance searing through silk.

Her face was pale, the smile she had forced upon it tightly stretched.

A small droplet of wine lay on her top lip. Once he might have leant over and licked it away, but he had never been a man to take a woman against her will and the wariness on Lucinda's face was easy to read. Drawing back, he opened the folder on the table beside him. There was a file fat with the transfer-of-ownership documents tucked inside the front cover. He pushed the papers across to her.

'I have signed the town house over to you already. The terms allow you sole use of the place until you die. Then it shall revert to our heir…or heirs if sins of the flesh are as enjoyable as I think you will find them to be.'

Worry brought lines to her forehead and the tip-tilt of her nose against the light made him look away. He remembered running his finger down the gentle slope and on to the plump rose of her lips. Once she had watched him as if he were the only man in existence. Once she had taken his breath away with a single stolen kiss. Now suspicion and wariness were the only expressions that he could read and the disappointment was disquieting.

'I have a pouch, too. A hundred pounds for the first time you lie with me and a hundred more for every time after that.' The heavy thud of the leather purse sounded on the file, like the promise of Antonio's flesh from the pen of Shakespeare. A pound for a pound. Payment for an heir.

Her teeth worried her bottom lip and shadowed eyes perused the bounty, but she did not reach out, leaving the largesse exactly where it was. Then she lifted her glass and had a generous gulp of wine before chancing a second and a third. Tay wanted to warn her of the strength of the draught, but in the circumstances he refrained. A relaxed Lucinda would be so much easier to handle than an angry one.

'So you are saying that when I become pregnant the bargain will be fulfilled?'

The catch in her voice nearly broke his will and for a moment he thought to nullify everything and walk away. 'A doctor will need to verify your condition, of course.'

'Like a brood mare,' she returned. Against the candlelight her pale hair shone and her eyes were back to flinty, fighting blue. During all his travels amongst the most beautiful women in the world he had never seen another like her.

He did not want her subdued. He wanted her like this. In bed she would be magnificent.

The thought had the flesh in his trousers swelling and he cursed, feeling like a boy again with no control over any of it. If he had any sense at all he would reach out now and strip her naked, demanding the rights all husbands received at the marriage altar and be done with any bargains. It was a God-given privilege, after all, and he had paid for her in blood and in gold.

He knew she saw the thought, too, for her hands tightened.

'I would never hurt you.' It was suddenly important that at least she knew that.

'Then let me go.'

'I can't.' Two words that stripped the life out of everything and his heart beat faster than ever it had during the bleak and lonely watches in the Americas when death could be forthcoming in one moment of inattention and often was. With care he reached out to gather a long curl of pale flaxen, turning it in his palm as the light caught wheat and gold and silver. 'I can only hope for release from the demons that have hounded us for three long years. Will you be brave enough to trust me?'

'Do I have any other alternative?'

He shook his head and the pulse at her throat slowed marginally—small signs of surrender.

To take the charade further he allowed her glance to escape from his own, falling out of contact. Eyes can take much from the soul, he thought, as she jammed her hands into the yellow silk of her skirt. He hoped dinner would be served soon. Eating would ease the tension that words were failing to do. How often had he plied an adversary with food and wine before picking the flesh of secrets clean away from the bone?

The thought that he did not wish to hurt Lucinda in any way at all left him struck dumb with shock.

Her innocence again and her goodness. He had had this same trouble in his bedchamber three years ago with the heady sighs of sexual release reverberating all around them—wholesomeness like some sharp-edged sword smiting evil with a conscience he had never felt so keenly before.

She was very warm. A fire burnt low in the grate, sending out a glow of red, and she was too hot even in her light clothing. She loosened her shawl. The scent of herbs wafted in the air around her. Lavender. She would never again smell the bloom without thinking of this moment, the documents and money spilled across the table before her, sordid rewards of lust.

'Marriage has left us both in a difficult position,' he continued, 'a no-man's land, if you like, precluding any other relationships we might wish to pursue. But if we use the situation wisely, we may at least enjoy it.'

The shock of his words made her draw in her breath. She was twenty-seven years old and, apart from one night three years ago, her sexuality had lain dormant and curdled.

Until now! Until a husband straight out of the

pages of some improper and implausible fairy tale had walked back into her life and demanded this.

The Duke of Alderworth was not soft or quiet or gentle. He was hard and strong and distant, his eyes devouring her and the lavender blurring her senses. When she shook her head he laughed and broke away.

'May the Lord above help us then if you think we might spin this out for all of a week, Duchess.'

Such brutal masculine honesty reminded Lucinda of her brothers and a further ache of homesickness claimed her. 'The trouble is that I do not know you at all, your Grace.' She had agreed to come to this place, agreed to the things he had said. She could not pull back now. But she did need time to adjust.

'I thought you had made it plain to everybody that you did. Intimately. Your three brothers at least will swear to it.'

'Much of what happened before the accident is lost to me,' she continued as if he had not spoken, 'though I know in my heart that you enjoyed far more than the mere kiss you acknowledge.'

He stood very still, watching her. 'More?'

'You wore no clothes.'

'I had retired for the night and you surprised me. There is no crime in that.'

'There were red marks upon my breasts.'

Laughter reverberated around the room, his face made years younger by mirth. She had not seen him like this before, humour sparkling and a dimple in one cheek.

'Fine breasts they were, too.'

Now he *was* lying, for she knew she had none of the form of those women of society whose charms were followed by the eyes of men.

'You think it cannot be so?' He walked across to her and traced his fingers down the line of her bodice, his touch running softly over the skin above the lace.

'You are a beautiful woman, Lucinda, and the pleasures of the flesh have their own reward.' The sensuality in his tone was beguiling and his touch made her draw in her breath. But she was neither gullible nor stupid.

'Lust is a base and shallow emotion, your Grace. It could never be enough to sustain a marriage.'

'You would want more?' He said this in such a way that Lucinda knew the thought of love had not occurred to him at all. Probably he found the softer emotions laughable—sensations that were as foreign to his world as easy and gratuitous sex would be to hers. The gap between them was a widening abyss.

'Hell and damnation,' he said, pushing back the hair on his forehead. Another opaque scar lay under the hairline and the anger on his face was unhidden.

Love.
She was speaking of that. He knew that she was and cold dread seeped through him.

Love only hurt. Enjoyment was better, of the mind or of the body it mattered not which. Enjoyment allowed the ease of parting when it was time to say goodbye and move on to the next place or person. Enjoyment was not the trap that love was.

Lord, he was paying his wife enough for such enjoyment and he was even biding his time to enable her to get used to the idea. He did not know of one single person who sustained their marriage in the way that Lucinda seemed to think was normal, the congeniality of two souls for ever linked.

This was the stuff of fairy tales and operas and the books that flooded out of the Minerva Press. He had read one once, just out of interest, and laughed at such an implausible nonsense.

His uncle had whispered the word in his ear, too, as he had hurt him. 'This is because I love you, Taylen. Only that.' The last time Tay had kicked the bastard hard in the balls as he had lunged for him and run to the door. The key hadn't turned, though, stuck in the lock as his fingers fumbled to release it and Hugo had caught him easily, holding his shaking body close and telling him he loved him over and over.

That was love. That was his memory of love, bound by blood and hurt to all the adults in his life, until one day they had simply washed their hands of him and sent him off to boarding school.

His deliverance. The few canings there were nothing compared to his regular and systematic abuse at

Alderworth, and in the summers when all the other boys save him returned home the masters had allowed him the free run of the place. To read. To walk. To fish.

Lucinda was watching him closely and it was disconcerting with his past rushing in between them.

'Our bargain consists of a hundred pounds each time you lie with me, the end coming when you conceive an heir.'

He knew such words would cut the talk of love to ribbons, but the sweat had begun creeping up his body. He needed to get away before she understood more about him than he wanted anyone to know and there was no kind way to say it.

He gathered the heavy leather pouch and the papers he had meant to have her sign. 'I find I am not hungry, Duchess. My servants will see to your evening meal.' With that he left her.

Chapter Twelve

A sound woke her, a groan muffled by something, but close. Lucinda sat up in bed and listened, the moon coming in through a gap in the curtains. It was night-time and late. She had spent a short time in the dining room and then retired upstairs as soon as she was able. She had seen no further sign at all of the Duke of Alderworth.

Another cry had her up on her feet and she walked to the door, placing her ear against the wood and listening. No footsteps hurried along the passageway, no hint of someone else hearing and helping. An owl called from the trees that marched in a line up a hill near the mansion, plaintive and lonely. Otherwise there was only silence.

Her feet were becoming cold on the parquet floor and she was about to get back into bed when a further sound came. This time she recognised the voice. Her hands opened the door and she was through it in a second, slipping through the unlocked door of the adjoining chamber. For a second dizziness made her clutch at the oak, this room familiar somehow and dangerous.

A candle burnt on a low bedside table and her husband was caught in a tangle of sheets, his hard body brown against the white, not asleep and not awake, but somewhere in a halfway place that was haunting.

'Wake up.' She shook him, the opened shirt he had on drenched in sweat, but his hand pushed her away. Not gently, either, but Lucinda had been raised in a house full of brothers and she pushed back.

'Wake up.' Louder now and more insistent. The bottle in front of him was drained and the smell of strong drink lingered around the room.

On the floor lay a book in Italian, the corners on one page turned down. A pile of other tomes in English, Italian and French sat in a nearby pile: Voltaire, Rousseau, Dante, Thomas Aquinas, Adam Smith and Machiavelli's *Il Principe*. Another flash of him reading this same book came to mind, the room draped in shadow save for a single candle. Before. She strained to recall other things, but could not.

'Taylen. Taylen. Wake up.' He came to in an instant, one moment boneless and the next ramrod stiff, the distant and vigilant Duke back in place.

The redness in his eyes was marked, the green of his iris darker against the colour. 'I shouted out?'

'Loudly. No one else came.'

Looking away, he reached for a fob watch positioned near the candle and checked the time. When his shirt dropped down a little as he stretched, Lucinda gasped. A whole row of scars slashed into the smoothness across the top of his back and she could barely believe the damage.

However, if he saw her looking he gave no sign of it, shrugging his shirt on further, fingers on the collar pinching both points of it inwards. His hands shook so much Lucinda thought that he would not be able to hold it closed.

All his rings had been stripped off, save their wedding ring and she wondered what that might mean. Sweat glistened on his face and his hair was plastered to his forehead, a worrying unsteadiness visible as he pushed himself up.

'Are you drunk?'

He laughed at that and shook his head. 'If only it was that simple…'

'Nightmares, then? When I was a child I had—' He stopped her with an impatient flick of his hand.

'I will ask Mrs Berwick to place you in another room in the morning. That way you will not be disturbed again.'

'This happens every night?'

'No.' He was so quick in his answer that Lucinda knew he lied.

'Exercise helped me. My mother insisted I rode each day for hours and after that I slept so much better at night.'

She could tell he was listening and so she carried on. 'I was a wilful child, you see, and always in trouble. My mother thought it would have been best had I been a boy, but I wasn't.'

A slight upturn of his lips had her carrying on.

'My brothers would be assigned each in turn to watch over me. Ashe and Taris were far older than I was and they took the duty seriously. Cristo was more my age and seemed to get in worse scrapes than even I was capable of. Alice was not a woman to be too bothered with children, you see. Her garden was her great love.'

'And your father? Where was he when all of this was going on?'

'Overseeing the running of the estate. Ensuring the lineage of the Wellinghams remained financially viable. He died of a heart condition when I was young. I would probably have been a disappointment to him had he lived.'

'Were I a father I would hold no impossible expectations of my children.'

A father! There it was again, that same old hint of why they were both here. She could see he also was reminded of the fact because his eyes turned smoky and he pushed himself up out of the bed.

He had fallen asleep in his clothes and his boots, the rumpled linen of his shirt sticking to his skin where the sweat had gathered. The nightmares had carved deep lines of desolation across his face. Almost as deep as those on his back. Could they be the marks of a careful and judicious beating administered to a child with as much hatred as was possible?

She held her breath with the enormity of it all, watching as he poured himself a generous glass of a drink that did not look alcoholic and finished the lot. Her nightgown felt insubstantial and she wished she had stopped to put on the matching negligee. Outside the moon was low and the night was dark, a mounting wind throwing the branch of a tree against the glass in his window.

'Tomorrow I shall take you riding…sedately.' For a moment she could not quite understand what it was he spoke of. Then she did.

'My mother will be smiling down from Heaven.'

'Or warning you away from me as all your brothers have done and hoping like hell that you heed her.'

'You keep on telling me that you are not safe.'

Walking to the window, he pulled back the curtain of heavy burgundy velvet.

'Come and look, Lucy.' It was the first time he had called her the name that her family did and she went across to him. He did not touch her, but positioned himself behind, his breath warm against her neck.

'As far as the eye can see it is Ellesmere land. From the hills against the sky here to the place where the moon shines on the lake there and behind the house a thousand acres yet again rising through the valleys. This is the safety that my father squandered and my mother cared not a jot for. This was the reason I took the money from your brother to disappear after our wedding. It was never meant as a slight to you.'

'A precious bequest?'

She felt him nod.

'If it were Falder I would have done exactly the same.'

'Thank you.' His hand came down upon her shoulder, the pressure gentle at first and then building as it slid across silk and shadow to rest on the sensitive skin at her neck. She wanted to lean in and keep him there, all the pent-up loneliness bursting forth into a simple need.

He was dangerous and difficult and menacing. He was also the only lawfully wedded husband she was ever likely to have. When he turned her slowly, the greenness in his eyes was darkened by half-light and gentle honesty, a man woken up by his past and trying to come to terms with his present.

His confession of faithfulness in the Beauchamps' salon made her braver and she brought her arms up around him. She could feel the welts of the old scars, the cotton in his shirt hiding nothing. Drawing one finger along the length of a twisted ridge, she suddenly had an image of the past. She had wanted him then as she did now.

'I remember pieces. I remember this.'

His only answer was his mouth upon hers and then she forgot everything as his tongue slanted inwards. Pure masculinity found her essence through touch and taste and she knew in the first second

of his onslaught exactly what it was all those society women who watched him through their hooded
glances had known.

He was both tempered steel and quicksilver, the
opposites melding wonderment and delight and he
wanted from her what men like him had wanted from
a woman through the centuries since the very beginning of time. The quiet kiss she had thought to offer
was overtaken by a storm of sensation.

There was no sense in it left, no moderation, no
limit on the depth of her feeling, no careful pru-
dence. All there was were heartbeats and warmth.
Unable to understand what was happening, she simply closed her eyes and let him take, the magic finally in her grasp.

Her bosom heaved as he moved closer, drawing
his thumb along the edge of her throat and across the
bones of her chest. When he sucked at his forefinger
and ran it fast over one nipple, she arched back, her
nightgown leaving nothing hidden, and the languid
glassy abandonment of passion showed in her eyes
before she closed them. His woman. Paid for and
bought. Legally bound until the very end of time.
No confines on anything. He could use her exactly
as he willed.

He wanted to rip away the rest of her clothes and
have her there now upon the floor, emptying himself
into her time and time again until there was nothing left of three years of desperation and urgency.

The more worrying thought that a woman like this could in some way inveigle herself into a corner of his heart confused him. He felt as if he could tell her things he never wanted another to know and break covenants that he had always kept.

Carefully he pushed her back, his thumb running across the soft line of one cheek and then the swelling of her lip. Bewilderment lay in her eyes, demanding explanation, but the nightmares always left him exhausted—too exhausted to deal with the complex labyrinth that was a relationship.

'Why is it like this between us?' Her question, dredged from the depths of need.

'I do not know, sweetheart, but now is not the hour to find out. It is time you were back in your bed.'

She looked away, pulling the silk of her gown back into place at her neck, a prim and proper covering of what had been there only a moment before. Her hair had escaped the loose plait she had worn when she had entered the room and fell in waves across her shoulders, the paleness caught between candle and moonlight and the length emphasising her slim height as it fell to the curve of her waist.

His fingers tightened against his thighs and he wished she would leave, shutting the door behind temptation because if she stayed much longer he did not trust himself enough not to reach out and remove any choice.

'Goodnight.' Her voice was strained and low and a few seconds later she was gone.

* * *

Lucinda sat on her bed, trying to catch her breath, her heart pounding in her chest.

She wanted him. She did. She wanted him to show her what it was that had boiled between them when he had kissed her. Her fingers traced down the line of her bodice, cupping one breast through the layers of fabric, feeling the same things that he had. The thought had her standing because she had never been a woman who was overtly sensual, the men in London society leaving her with no true desire other than a residual and slight interest in what happened between the sexes. Nothing more.

Until now.

Different. Alive. Aching everywhere. For him. The skin around her nipples tightened as she imagined his mouth upon them, the place between her legs throbbing in anticipation. The jade Emerald had bequeathed her lay between her breasts. For happiness, her sister-in-law had promised. She wondered what this emotion she felt now was. Certainly there was an excitement that was foreign and wonderful.

Could one be married in lust and not in love?

Would that be enough?

Or might the agreements between them eventually ignite the sort of marriage her brothers had, the forever-and-ever sort that lasted through thick and thin?

Her husband did not seem to think so and yet he had kissed her in a way that made no sense of the distance he offered. His heart had raced as fast as hers, she had felt it where their skin had touched, the heat in his eyes belying the aloofness he brokered.

When he had stood behind her at the window, offering an explanation why he took money from her brother, she could almost imagine him standing there as a loving husband who cared for her feelings and who wanted her to understand that it was not insult but truth he sought.

She wiped away the tears in her eyes with the back of her hand, a quick angry movement because such a maudlin wallowing was useless.

She had been lonely for years, lost in her own company amidst a family who all had partners. The shared glances, the careful smiles, the way a hand was given in complicit understanding. These were the things she had never discovered, never desired until now.

The moonlight drew mottled, patterned trails across her skin, paleness overlaid by shadow. The artist in her enjoyed the line and the beauty of the design, but the woman only saw the desolation of solitude.

How would she be able to go through with this bargain of conceiving an heir if every part of her wanted so much more than he would give?

Chapter Thirteen

Lucinda spent the morning on her own. There had been no sign of her husband at all, no movements from his room. She knew this because she had been listening most carefully, getting up to place her head against the door at any sign of noise.

Mrs Berwick bustled in just before twelve.

'The master was asking after you, your Grace.'

'The Duke is up already?'

'Indeed. Riding across the top valley would be my guess, on that black horse of his that goes like the wind.'

Lucinda crossed to the wardrobe to find her bonnet and coat. Within a moment she was on the front portico, Mrs Berwick pointing out the formal gardens and the small pathway to the Ellesmere stables.

Finally she was alone, the wind on her face and the sun appearing from time to time between ominous banks of high, dark cloud.

A dog joined her on her walk a little way into the tumbled-down garden, his coat mangy and his head hanging. She could not even make a guess as to its pedigree, for the animal had the head of a Labrador, the body of a much thinner hound and the hairiest and longest of legs. Usually she was frightened of dogs, as she had been bitten badly once at Falder and had not been much in their company since, but this animal with its trusting brown eyes, its odd shape and a tail that curled twice before tucking under its back legs was so comical it was comforting. All day she had been alone, so when the animal's wet muzzle came into the curl of her fingers she laughed.

'Who are you?' Her voice brought it to a stop.

'His name is Dog.' Taylen Ellesmere was suddenly behind her, his riding clothes splattered with mud and no sign on his face at all to indicate he had any memory of last night. Perhaps he had felt nothing. Perhaps for him the kiss had been like one of the many others he had bequeathed to countless beautiful women across his lifetime.

'Is he yours?' Lucinda hoped that the rush of heat on her cheeks did not show.

'My carriage almost ran him over on the London riverfront and so I had him brought up here.'

'When?'

'The first day I arrived back in England, a month and a half ago now. It seemed a sign,' he added, an unexpected lopsided smile having a strange effect on the area around her heart.

'A sign of what?'

'A sign indicating that I was meant to stay. An anchor, if you like.'

'Mrs Berwick told me you had concentrated your efforts on bringing the farm cottages up to a habitable standard.'

'The estate needs work, though there are some who do not like what I am trying to accomplish.'

'Change always polarises people. Asher says that often.'

He smiled, and nodded. 'In a year I could have Alderworth profitable again…' He stopped, a sense of wariness in the words. 'But you probably have no interest in such things?'

His query trembled into the space between them.

'On the contrary. If this is to be my home, I could help you.'

'Our home.'

And just like that she was back again into breathlessness, enchantment shimmering in the air between them.

'Do you have your riding clothes?'

'Of course.'

'Then come with me and I will show you Alderworth from the hills.'

'Now?'

Nodding, he called the dog back to his side, its mangy spine rising into his hand where he patted it.

'Give me ten minutes,' she answered before breaking into a brisk walk.

* * *

Taylen stood and watched her leave, desire seeping into a cold dread.

Hugo Shields seemed to reach out from the grave and deny him any thoughts of hope, years after he had died with a bullet through his heart. His uncle had gone into his afterlife muttering the threats he'd made such an art form of whilst living, insults softening into pleas and then whimpers as the life blood had run from him. Tay had allowed him no forgiveness, simply watching with distaste and relief as he took his last and final breath. The Italian nobleman, who had shot Hugo as a card cheat, had taken ship back to the Continent that very night and a youthful Taylen had never spoken of the incident to anyone.

Secrets and lies. It was who he was, what he had become, and no amount of longing could change it. It was why the nightmares never left him, but spun into the release of sleep like a spider gathering corpses. He could not hide the darkness inside him from Lucinda and if he tried to…

He shook his head. He would have to be honest, for he owed her at least that.

The dog's whining made him tense.

With her riding habit in place Lucinda rejoined Taylen at the front of the stables.

The large black horse she had seen at a distance from the window of her room was twice as impressive close up. She stayed a good ten feet away from him as she looked over the lines of his body.

'He is beautiful. What do you call him?'

'Hades. My father brought his grandsire out from France after winning a lucrative hand of faro.'

Taylen Ellesmere never seemed cowed by scandal; rather he threw any caution in the face of the wind and challenged comment. Attack was better than any defence. He used the maxim like an expert.

'Your family is unusual.'

'There isn't much of it left.'

'The very opposite of mine, then. Sometimes I used to think there were too many Wellinghams, but now...'

She trailed off, but he finished the sentence for her. 'Now when you see the alternative it makes you realise how lucky you are?'

'I think that is true. They are not so bad, you know, my brothers. It is only that they are trying to protect me.'

'From further ruin?' He smiled unexpectedly, the green in his eyes paler today than she had ever seen it. The Dissolute Duke who watched over his estate out of a duty he could have refused, but didn't.

Sometimes her husband was so very like her brothers. Confusion made her ramble.

'It is good to be away from town and Alderworth is a beautiful place despite the disrepair or perhaps because of it, I think, although I can imagine my mother's displeasure at the state of your garden.'

'I would be more than happy if you wish to oversee any repair, Lucinda.'

She laughed. 'Gardening being such a quiet and docile hobby…'

'At least it might stop you from galloping *ventre à terre*.'

She knew he would kiss her before he leaned over. She could see it in the way his face softened, humour changing to some other thing less discernible. As the wind lifted her riding skirt and blew the falling leaves into eddies around their feet, she simply closed her eyes and felt his warmth against hers and his solidness, his fingers on the skin of her arm, stroking down to catch her to him, no questions left. Just them with a beautiful horse standing behind, the yellow sandstone of the stables pitted with age and the peace of the early afternoon settling in.

This kiss was different from the one they had shared the night before. This kiss came with all the knowledge of what they both wanted—nay, what they needed from each other.

They came together with a hard edge of disbelief, thrown into a storm of movement, his hand around the back of her head, his body pressed against her own. This time she did not limit what she gave in return, her teeth biting down and tasting the power of abandon. She was not careful or circumspect or quiet. She was all woman released from the fetters of years of manners and demeanour that denoted a

Wellingham daughter, the expectations of society a distant and unpleasant memory.

She could no longer care. Her fingers wound through his hair as his tongue came inside her mouth, rough and urgent, no quiet asking in it as he held his hands on each side of her face.

This was what she wanted, the taking and taking, moulded into desire, the loss of self in a thrall that held no end. A moment or an hour? It was his choice. She would have lain down upon the grass beneath the roses if he had asked her, opening to him, accepting the roaring release of a womanhood for ever tied to agreements and conditions and plain cold reason. Respecting the fact that he was a man caught in the complexities of family and trying to make the best of it, she could deny him nothing.

Nothing. Her mouth widened as he came within, tilting her, his breath hoarse and raw, his thumb on the nape of her neck as she arched back and simply enjoyed.

He could not remember ever revelling in the company of another as much as he did his wife. He had never had a confidante before, a person who might guard his back against the world despite everything that was said of him. The wonder of it was humbling.

Lucinda kissed like the most skilled of all courtesans, allowing him things most ladies didn't, gentle softness dispensed with under a building and aching need. When her teeth came down on his lip he smiled, the pain of it inciting urgency as he took her breath into his own, swallowing her air and exchanging it for his. He bound her mouth in a tight seal of authority, pressing down so that she had to trust him. She did not fight, though her eyes flew open, watching, glazed into submission, waiting while he fed her breath.

He had never felt such a compelling insistence for any woman, not in all the years of his life enjoying the fruits of a reputation he had earned at the hands of parents who taught him not to care for anything or anyone. So very easy to take and to leave.

But with Lucinda there was a betrothal that was impossible to break before man and before God, the edicts written in the law of the land and handed down through many centuries of union.

Unions that produced the next generations, heirs who could hold the great estates in the palms of their hands and care for their longevity as no outsider would ever be able to.

His heirs. Their heirs. The children of Alderworth who would follow in his footsteps. An agreement bound by time and gold.

Breaking away from her, he ran his hands through his hair and swore. This was not how it was supposed to be, this desperate need to be inside her, a sense of for ever in his thoughts that was as scary as it was impossible.

No one had ever stayed at his side through thick and thin, through richer and poorer, through the vagaries of trouble and the inadequacy of laws. No one at all, save Lance Montcrieff, who had died trying to show him such friendship was possible even as the last piece of life had bled from him, warm on the dusty turnings of earth and in a land that was far from home.

His breath felt shaky and he turned from his wife's sky-blue gaze, not wanting her to see things he had shown to no one before. Give a little of yourself and be punished for it. Trust another and that emotion would be thrown back as corruption and abuse. Or loss.

After his grandmother's betrayal he had allowed his uncle to see his vulnerability when he had come to collect him from the hospital in Rouen. Then another sort of deception had begun, one worse than his grandmother's heavy hand, one wrapped in soft bare flesh and whispered words. It was then he had understood that love equalled pain and shame. When he had finally rid himself of his uncle's depravities he had found a different enjoyment of the flesh. One that required neither trust nor honesty. One that allowed him the freedom to move on from a woman before there was ever the chance of more than a way to pass the hours of his life, superficial, numerous and unimportant.

'I know there is a lot I need to learn about the art of kissing…?'

He stiffened as he faced her, hating the worry so evident in her voice.

'But I no longer wish to wait to make an heir. I want to know where a kiss like that one might lead to next, Taylen. I am twenty-seven years old and I do not wish for another single day to pass before I know.'

Raw and honest with her chest heaving, Lucinda reminded him of everything that was good in the world.

'Now?' He did not recognise his own voice.

She nodded, a small hint of nerves, but still she stood before him, unflinching.

Tay could not believe she might mean it and yet in the aftermath of their kiss his body had hardened and risen. He took the chance of waiting no longer by simply holding out his hand.

Her fingers laced about his own, intertwined.

'Come, then.'

Calling to his man to unsaddle Hades, he strode back through the gardens along the white shell paths, ten steps and then twenty, always assuming that she would pull away. She did not.

He walked through the main salon at the bottom of the house, the servants watching them, a strange juxtaposition of the normal and the absurd.

A bargain.

A payment.

An heir.

He had never felt as he did at that moment, leading his wife towards his bedchamber and knowing what would happen once they got there.

Mrs Berwick asked him a question and he answered, the warmth of Lucinda's fingers burning need into his soul. He saw his wife's eyes were lowered lest the truth of what lay inside was seen. Speaking in words that were empty, his mind replayed other words, stronger words, words that would change both of their lives for ever. He felt as if they were tied by a quivering single thread, its quicksilver need running through all the parts of him. Forcing him on.

Up the stairs they climbed, Lucinda's breath strained. Not from exertion, but from anticipation. He almost smiled then, although humour was far from what he felt.

Then through the door they went, the heavy oak of it shutting behind them and the locks turning. The noise elicited a small involuntary flinch from Lucinda, but she did not speak. Pocketing the key, he moved away, dropping the contact, needing the space. For the first time in a life filled with indulgence and dissoluteness he did not know where to begin.

His wife did it for him, undoing her jacket buttons one by one, her small hands mesmerising. The shirt beneath was of the finest linen, inset with lace, her flesh peeking through where the pattern of the stitches changed. He stepped forwards.

'Let me?'

She nodded, stood still as he drew her hair into his hands and released the mass of gold and wheat from restraint, running his fingers through the curls so that they were freed from the heavy chignon. He wanted to see her tresses against her pale skin, enveloping the curve of her breasts and hips. He wanted to lay her down upon his bed and mould the shape of her to his so that she would never forget him, marked and branded.

The racing beat of her heart belied the bravado she was showing him as he undid the small mother-of-pearl buttons that held the last of her bodice together.

He had done this before, in this very room three years ago, unlaced Lucinda and understood the beauty beneath the cloth, but this time was different. This time she was his wife, promised to him, bound in law and troth and honour.

Marriage. His parents had never venerated the spirit of such a union, but to him... He stopped.

Not empty words after all. The wedding ring he wore glinted in the light, catching gold.

'Only for an heir...?' She phrased this in a question, running her tongue around the dryness of her lips as her head tilted back.

Asking for more.

He pulled the cloth away and her breasts fell out into his gaze, then his hands lay across them, the fullness firm and pale.

Lust ruled now, heating blood, shallowing breath, raising skin. His mouth came around one rose-hued peak and he sucked, hard, the burn of want and need, the ache of completion, the trembling primeval blaze.

She groaned and he kneaded the other nipple, the thread between them snaking into hardness, snaring desire.

'Now.'

Her voice, and no longer a question. Raising his head, he simply picked her up, her bodice trailing downwards and the skirt she wore pulled up across his arms, the dainty beauty of her ankles and shins on show.

She did not fight him, but lay still as he placed her on his bed. No resistance. His hands came beneath her skirt, into the silk of her petticoats, under the thin nothingness of her drawers. Until only skin remained, thick and swollen and soft feminine skin, wet with her wanting.

'It may hurt, my love.' He had to warn her as he unbuttoned his trousers. She did not look at his nakedness, for her eyes were closed now, the quiet blush of need on her cheeks, the trembling, too, of something unknown. He wished he could find the words that she wanted him to give her, but the truth was more important.

'I need you, Lucinda. I need all of you.'

At that she opened her eyes, acquiescence and knowledge now in the blue as one arm reached out to caress the planes of his stomach before falling lower. An elemental virgin-siren, the release of her breath heard in the quietness, a thin line of beaded sweat on the top of her lips.

Kicking off his boots and trousers, he lifted her

skirt and opened her legs, the searing flesh of his manhood stilling as his fingers parted heat—balanced, waiting, poised on that moment of change that comes to every new bride.

Slipping inwards, driving hard, breaking flesh as she arched up to him, slick in the coupling. Her hands tried to push him away, her nails digging into his back, the terror of it written into one single keening cry. And then stillness as he waited, engorged, filling her, tightening, the deep pain of loving changing into a different consciousness.

Her breath came quick now, the dead weight of him pinning her down, unmoving.

'Wait, sweetheart.' It was all he could say. Wait until we become accustomed to each other. Wait until your body answers. Wait until the waves of response begin.

And then they did. A slight quiver of flesh, an easing, a softening, the first call of her body as she moved and allowed him a different access. Slowly. Out and in again. Deeper. Faster. Wider. Harder. Again. And again. He prayed that the pain was lessening and changing into some life-filled thrall that was indescribable and heightened. He knew that he had her when her hands came around his back and she held him to her as if she might never let him go.

She could neither breathe nor think. Every part of her was centred in the place between her legs where he was in her, joined by flesh, the hurt leaving now, not as ragged, and another pain building. A different pain. One that held her stiff and breathless, reaching for what was promised.

One that made her shake and groan and stretch as his movements quickened, needing the beauty of it, feeling the togetherness of what brought a man and a woman into a single person, nothing between them save the knowledge of each other. His breath against her throat, the movements faster now, reaching up and racing against hope and heat and desperate need.

And then a release, a melting ache of absolution quivering through the stiffness, widening and deepening, rolling across her stomach inside everything. She shouted out, her voice heard far away, the beaching waves unlike anything she had ever felt or known.

Lost in sensation. Adrift. Satisfied. Crying. Her tears hot on her cheeks and brushed away softly by a husband who had astonished her.

She heard the thundering of her heart inside her head, a languid lethargy in her limbs, the weight of Taylen and the heat of him drawing energy away.

Still joined. She could feel him twitch, the thick engorgement inside. Sweat ran through all the places between them.

'Thank you.' His words, caught between deep breaths.

Smiling, she closed her eyes, unable to say more, tears drying tight against her cheeks. She wanted to stay here just like this in the silence, wrapped inside each other's skin, the sun slanting across the room in a yellow curtain of light.

Heaven.

'I always wondered why my brothers were so… happy being married. Does everyone feel this?' She had to know, had to understand.

'No. My parents hated each other with a passion.'

'So they sent you away?' She watched him, his body bare in the light, the edges of the marks on his back creeping round on to his ribs. One finger traced a scar in wordless question.

'On occasion. And when I was here they ignored me,' he said, watching the ceiling, and Lucinda knew from the tone in his voice that the things he was thinking had been stored inside him for a long, long time.

'Lady Shields's maid said that you were in hospital in France?'

'In Rouen. My grandmother hurt me when we were on holiday there. I had asked one of her friends if I could live with them, you see, and she found out and was furious. But it was only after my uncle came to pick me up a good month later that I understood the true meaning of…brutality.'

He whispered the word, softly, anger leaving him stiff and motionless. 'My mother's brother decided I needed lessons in…obeying him and took such tutorship to heart.' He looked at her then full in the eyes, the torment of memory bright and fierce.

'I was twelve years old and my parents had both

died the previous summer. Twelve is no age to fight back, you see…and I couldn't. He…he…'

Shaking her head, she placed her fingers on his lips as if to stop what he might say next. 'I love you, Taylen. I love you because the things you have been through have made you who you now are. Strong. Certain. I think I must have always loved you, even then, when we first met, even without the memory of it.'

A single tear traced its way down the side of her face and he kissed it away before covering her lips and taking all that she said inside of him. Again.

Tay watched her as she fell asleep, lost safe in the arms of dreaming. Her lashes were long and curled, the tips dipped in lightness and even in slumber her dimples were still apparent. Three years of waiting for her and he had ruined it with his stupid truth-fulness.

He slipped away from her body and sat on the bed, the blood of sacrifice easily seen on the top of his thighs.

How could she love him after the things he had told her? How could she find it in herself to do that? Maybe now it was possible in the first flush of passion, but tomorrow when the truth settled? What might happen then?

Every confessed word had been wrong and heavy and he swallowed twice, guilt rising with anger as he fumbled with the drawer to one side of his bed and extracted a hundred pounds.

Hers for the bargain.

He placed the notes carefully upon the counterpane and did not look back again as he stood to collect his garments and leave the room.

In the morning he rode to the home of Lance Montcrieff's wife a good five miles from Alderworth. He had installed Lance's widow in one of his smaller estates since his friend's death when she had been ousted from her home by the heir and had visited her a number of times since returning to England a month and a half ago. He knew that Elizabeth Montcrieff wanted more from him than he could give and part of the reason he needed to see her this morning was to put an end to the hopes of any type of relationship between them.

Lance had loved his wife, well and truly, and Tay knew that his friend would have wanted his family to be settled and secure. Without any other relatives to help her, he felt she was his responsibility.

The butler took him straight through into the library and he was greeted almost immediately by Elizabeth.

'I did not know you were coming this morning, Duke.' The velvet in her voice was smooth. On her lips was the lightest of colour. The heavy perfume she favoured filled the air between them.

'There is a chance of leasing a town house in London, Elizabeth. It is central and there is a school just around the corner suitable for the girls. I think you would be happy there with the chance of more society and a wider group of people to talk to.'

She watched him intently. 'I hear that your wife has arrived at Alderworth. It is the only topic of conversation one hears at the moment around here.'

Her brown eyes were resigned, her smile calm. She was not a woman given to histrionics and she was sensible enough to understand he did not wish for tears.

'I am sorry if I have given you any cause to think there could have been something more between us…'

'You have not, Duke. You have been most circumspect and generous.'

'It was Lance's final wish as he died. He made me promise to look after you, but life has changed and my wife is…' He stopped. What was Lucinda to him? A mother for his child? Or much, much more?

Her hand came down across his own. 'I understand. You have helped me with a home and a living, Duke, and for that I shall be for ever grateful. You have done your duty ten times over.' Unshed tears banked in her eyes. 'I could not have wished for a more thoughtful man in the face of my own loss and loneliness. I hope her Grace knows what a treasure she has in you.'

He smiled at her words. 'My lawyer says that you have not touched the money I deposited into your account.'

'I have not needed to. Everything has been pro-vided for me here. But now…' She hesitated. 'Now I think I will repair to London and see what that town has to offer us. You have been more than generous and I will always be grateful.'

'Nay. It was Lance's share.'

She shook her head. 'I know the real money did not come in until after his death when you diversified into other areas. I am certain that you know that, too.'

Elizabeth Montcrieff had never looked so beau-tiful to him, a woman of honour and integrity. He hoped that she would find what it was she needed from London and that somewhere in the future he might bring Lucinda to meet her.

'There is one more thing,' he said as he turned to leave. Reaching into his pocket, he extracted the ring Lance had worn in Georgia and handed it to her. 'This should be yours.'

He laid the gold in her palm. *LM.* The initials of his first real friend. But now he had another. The thought came from nowhere, but the truth of it was undeniable.

Lucinda.

Suddenly exhaustion overtook everything. He wanted to be away from this house and out in the open again, feeling the wide space of freedom over his head and the chance of redemption in his heart. He couldn't go home, not just yet. He needed the hope of Lucinda's words for a while longer, unspoilt by the consideration that must blossom when she had time to think about all that he had told her.

Saying goodbye to Elizabeth, he rode for the village to buy a drink.

Chapter Fourteen

'His Grace has been called away to one of his other properties, your Grace.'

Mrs Berwick gave her the information as Lucinda came down to the dining room for breakfast.

'Did he say when he would return?' Lucinda kept her voice even and controlled, though her hand shook as she helped herself to bacon and eggs.

'No. He did not. Sometimes it is a few days before he is back, but this time...?' The housekeeper left the question unanswered.

'I see.'

And she did.

Taylen Ellesmere had run from Alderworth as fast as he had been able to even with her ill-given exclamation of love. It was the blood. Her blood. Her virgin blood of pure deceit. He had been trapped into a marriage, beaten by her brothers and forced into years in a far-off land with no hope of return and all because of lies. She knew that now, the proof of it on the bed sheets and in the soreness between her legs. He had never touched her there.

It was her husband who had held her neck still after the accident and made certain that the damage was not worse. She remembered that, too, the paleness of his face above her as he had strained to keep her immobile, the cold rain streaming down upon him and shattered glass in all of the broken and damaged lines of his skin.

Every single thing he had told her family had been true about the lack of relationship between them and she had sacrificed him because of it.

Only an heir. She understood the words now as she had not before. An heir from the only wife he was ever likely to have and all because of her lies. The notes on her bed when she awakened came to mind, spread out beside her. It looked a lot when counted in falsehoods.

But other thoughts also surfaced. The secrets that he had shared with her last night were not easy or small truths, the gift of confidence surprising and humbling. He had laid his soul at her feet even as anger had marked his eyes, brittle, shameful fury stained in green and he had not turned away when she said that she loved him.

One hand strayed to her stomach. *Please let his seed take. Please, please let a child grow.*

She prayed for that with all her heart.

She wanted him back. She wanted to tell him that

her lie had been sorely mistaken and that she was sorry. She wanted to hold him against the hurt of his youth, in her arms away from the loss of an innocence that should have been safeguarded.

But he would not come and the only companion left to her was the unkempt dog who followed her back to her room.

'I am not certain if you are allowed in here,' she said in the lowest of voices, for she had already seen the animal being shooed out a number of times today. Kneeling, she offered her hand to him and he sidled over, his tail fixed as it always was between his legs.

'Are you hurting?' The query had her placing her fingers upon the matted hoary coat and wondering what other care the animal had missed out on. Perhaps he was more like his master than she had originally thought, tossed out from home and beaten.

She reached for one of her brushes and began to try to untangle the knots. Surprisingly a coat that was both lighter and longer began to emerge, the dog looking more and more presentable with each stroke.

'Like a swan,' she said to him and laughed as he lay down, his body comforting against her own. 'If you were mine, I should call you Swan.'

The sudden and unexpected sounds of feet moving along the corridor outside made her stiffen as the door-handle turned. Her husband appeared, dressed in his riding cape with a hat in hand.

His eyes went to the dog, a frown lingering as he called to the animal. It stood instantly and walked across to stand beside him, the bony ridge of its back prominent.

'He followed me in here.' It was all that Lucinda could say, banal and hackneyed, she knew, but her tongue was tied and she could not decide how to greet him, a stranger who had been a lover and was now back in the guise of a man who looked…unknown.

Confusion and ire surfaced and as he came closer she scrambled upright. A strong perfume was evident on his clothes.

'Thank you for last night, Lucinda.'

Another flush of red crawled up into her face. If he would not castigate her over her mistake, then surely it behoved her to mention it.

'My memory was faulty after the accident in the carriage. I believed that you had…enjoyed more than I wanted to offer.'

'And now?'

'Now in the light of yesterday I can see that I was mistaken in my accusations.' She made herself hold his glance. 'It cannot have been easy to have had your reputation so unkindly maligned and for that I apologise.'

He smiled, his skin creasing at the corner of his eyes, an outdoor man, a man who did not bother too much with the fripperies of fashion. 'My reputation was maligned a long time before you added to it. What do you remember?'

'Running into your room. You were reading and

naked. I remember that clearly. Machiavelli in Italian? I thought you had kissed me?'

'I did.'

'I also think you might have touched me.' She raised a hand and placed it across her breast. 'Here.'

'That, too.' His right hand joined hers, cold from the morning outside. She shivered and his other fingers drew a line down her cheek. 'I touched you like this,' he offered, 'and like this,' he added, cupping the flesh under her bosom. Even through the material of her gown her blood began to pump.

'And I wanted you to?'

He nodded.

'You must have hated me then, after my brothers told you I had said that you ruined me?'

Only for an heir. Only for an heir.

'I do not hate you.'

'But the payment you left on the bed. Is that only what this is?'

He stopped her questions simply by holding her against him, tightly bound, his jacket sprinkled with rain and wet.

'Last night…the things I told you…' He stopped, holding her close with the dog around their feet. She could not see his eyes or his face, but she could hear the beat of his heart against her ear.

When he did not speak she began to. 'Everyone has their secrets, Taylen. I ran away with a man when I was seventeen. Emerald, my brother's wife, stopped me before I boarded a ship and married him. It would have been a huge scandal if anyone else had known.'

'But they did not?'

'My brothers hushed it up and nothing else was ever said. I saw him again about five years later and thanked the Lord that I had been caught.'

'That bad?'

'He became a dandy, a man who enjoyed puce waistcoats and powdered hair. I doubt he thought of anything else at all. Then when I was twenty-two I fancied myself in love with another swain who turned out to be married already and just wanted a… dalliance. He was Italian, you see, and had not mentioned his family circumstances.'

'How did you find out?'

'My brothers never liked him and they sent a runner to Rome. I cried for a week until I understood that it was my fault really that any of these things had happened. After that, until I met you, I was quite circumspect. And when you left after our wedding I was virtually a recluse.'

'I wrote to you three times from Georgia, but you never replied. Did Cristo not give you my letters?'

'He did, Duke, but all you talked about in them were the environs where you now found yourself and a duty message was not what I wanted at all. So I decided that it was in my best interests never to think of you again.'

'You did not think I would come back to you?'

Lucinda breathed out. Every day she had hoped

it. Every day she had held her breath and wondered would it be this day that Taylen Ellesmere might come home. To her.

The knock at her door had them both turning, however, as the butler appeared in the doorway.

'Mrs Moncrieff is here, your Grace, and it seems that one of her daughters has gone missing. I have placed her in the blue salon.'

'Thank you. I will come down.' Anxiety covered Taylen's words as he accompanied his servant from the room. Not knowing whether to follow or to stay, Lucinda hesitated and her husband was gone from her sight even as she tarried.

Montcrieff. Was that not the name of Taylen's partner in the gold mine in Georgia? Shutting the door behind her, she made her way down the stairs after them.

In the blue salon she found a beautiful woman weeping in her husband's arms, her head against his breast.

'Emily has not returned from the Partridges and I sent a servant for her but there was no sign at all. When you came to me, Duke, I think she overheard that we might be leaving Tillings and going to London and she has made friends here and did not wish to go.'

She burst into noisy sobs and Lucinda could only stand and watch the spectacle like an outsider. The same perfume that had hung heavily on her husband's clothes was in this room as well.

She could see both the lines of guilt on his forehead and the familiar way the woman curled into his strength. Elizabeth Montcrieff wore his ring, too, she noticed, on the third finger of her left hand, the gold engraving glittering in the light.

Betrayal? Every part of her body wanted to deny what she was seeing, but she could not. Turning back to her room, she raced up the stairs as if a ghost was on her tail.

'I do not hate you.' He had said those very words not ten minutes before, but he did not love her, either. Not enough. For all his fine words, perhaps he was a cheat. A man with as many mistresses as he had years still to live; so many, in fact, that here was one straying into their very home, a demi-wife with his ring on her finger to prove the commitment.

She was glad for the key Taylen Ellesmere had given her and, locking her door against any intrusion, she tried to think of just exactly what she would do next.

Elizabeth held him as she might once have held her husband and as Tay tried to disengage her grip he saw a quick flash of a dark dress.

Had Lucinda come down the stairs behind him? Had she seen Elizabeth entwined about him and sobbing? Lord, if she had, she might imagine other things, too.

With a real effort he moved away from Lance's widow and poured her a brandy.

'Drink this. It will help.'

Thankfully she did swallow the draught without question and the tormented and hysterical crying stopped.

'If I have lost her, too…'

'You won't have. Emily will have gone to one of her friends' place to hide or to wait and see what you do as a result of it.'

Hope flared in dark eyes. 'You think she might have?'

'I do.'

The sobbing began again, quieter though now. 'She has been difficult since her father's death and I have not been as strong as I have needed to be.'

'Then take a lesson and begin in London, Elizabeth. The school there is a good one and the girls will have all the care and direction they require. A new start is exactly what you all need.'

'Could you come back to Tillings with me now and talk to her, when we have found her? She listens to you just as she used to listen to her father.'

Tay's heart sank. He knew that it would be dark before he could return home to Alderworth. He was also worried about Lucinda, but with a carriage waiting outside and an anxious mother inside he had no time to go upstairs and explain everything to her.

Tomorrow he would take his wife out riding and show her the estate. Perhaps if she was willing he could also take her back to his bedchamber and find the same magic that they had discovered last night.

* * *

It was already morning. Lucinda had fallen asleep fully dressed under the cover of a thick blanket that lay at the bottom of her small bed after waiting nearly half the night to see whether Taylen would return.

But he had not come home. He had gone with the beautiful dark-haired woman and as the hours had tumbled one across the other she knew that he would not be back. She felt sick with the implications of what that might mean.

Had he left again, this time with the full intent never to return? My God, her brothers had been right. Exactly right. She should have heeded their word and refused to accompany him to his estate. Once a snake, always a snake. Yet he hadn't been that at all. He had been honest and honourable. It had been her memory at fault and he was the one who had suffered.

A knock on the door had her sitting up, running the back of her hand quickly against her eyes and trying to place a smile where anguish had just been.

'May I come in? I have your breakfast tray.'

Scrambling up, Lucinda unlocked the door and a maid came bustling in with freshly baked rolls and a pot of tea.

'Mrs Berwick said I was to tell you that the master will be a-riding home this morning from the direction of the local village, your Grace. She said that the groom could find you a mount should you wish to venture out and meet him.'

The idea appealed. A ride might blow away the cobwebs Lucinda felt building and give her freedom to think. The added bonus was that meeting him out in the open would allow them to talk in private.

If she got one of the stable hands to show her the way she would not get lost and the weather outside looked finer than it had in weeks. When the dog came through the door she decided to take him, too, reasoning that the exercise would be good for the hound.

The horses standing in the stables were by and large older hacks, though one smaller filly caught her attention.

'What of that one?' she asked the stable boy. 'The roan mare at the end?'

'Her name is Venus. She's a mite skittish in temperament, though, for she came with his Grace's black as a pair and when Hades is gone she's apt to fret.'

The perfect ride, then. If she had any chance of meeting up with the returning Duke, the odds had just got better.

'Who usually takes her out?'

Silence told her that nobody did.

'I can saddle up a more docile horse if you would rather, your Grace.'

'No. This one will be fine.' Lucinda liked the lines of Venus and she felt desperate for a good long stretch. None of the other horses here looked as if they would give her any more than a slow canter.

With anticipation she mounted and was surprised by the docile way the horse allowed her a seat. The day was blue and it had been a while since she had sat on the back of a horse in the countryside and raced across the land, feeling the wind in her hair and liberty in her veins.

After all that had happened she needed to simply feel. The wonderment in such an unexpected loving still left every fibre in her body alive with promise and had her heart racing.

She had lain there when she had awoken and felt…different. A woman who understood exactly what it was that others spoke of in the hushed tones on the far side of rooms. Yet now with Taylen's absence everything had returned to only bewilderment.

Veering left at the main gate as the stable boy had directed, she allowed Venus her head, racing across the line of fence and bush with the sun on her shoulders. The silence of the place was absolute, the birdsong long since diminished and the day shaping up into a glorious one. The dog loped at her side in an easy gait.

At the top of the incline the lands of Alderworth spread out around her as a tableau and Lucinda wished she had brought her drawing things to capture such a view. Her eyes searched out the paths coming in from all directions, but there was nothing. Perhaps Tay had stayed on longer, lying entwined in the arms of the beautiful widow, and regretting the confidence he had allowed in his marriage bed.

A brace of loud shots had her turning as a group of men burst from the trees a good five hundred yards away.

Hunters. Lucinda felt the quiver of her horse's fright even before she bolted, whipping the reins from her hands and tearing off in the opposite direction from where they had appeared.

She could only hang on, her fingers entwined in the hair of the mane and her feet solid in the stirrups. A hundred yards and then two, the hilly terrain giving way to a long valley and trees. The branches whipped her face as she tried to stop, shouting at her horse to slow as hooves beat faster against the muddy ground. Then she was off, flying through the air with the rush of landscape beside her and down on to the slope of a gully. She might well have stopped if there had not been a disused well at the bottom, the slopes rolling into the mouth of it and over into darkness.

A good six feet down she clung to the roots of a tree and tried to force her body into the space between earth and wood. Already she felt sick, disorientated, dizzy. Pain brought her back to the moment and the last thing she remembered was the dog looking down before turning away from the gap in the sky, the sound of his panicked barking disappearing on the wind.

One of the lads came out to meet him as Taylen cantered in to the stables. He had left the village as early as he could and made excellent time back to

Alderworth. Looking at his timepiece, he saw it to be twenty minutes short of twelve. Emily had been reunited with her mother after a number of hours of searching and was suitably apologetic, though with a night behind him in the local inn Tay was glad to leave and head for home.

A sort of panic had gnawed at him for hours, the idea that something was not quite right pervading all his thoughts.

'Will you be joining her Grace out riding, your Grace?' The young stable hand's face was tinged with worry.

'The Duchess has taken out one of the horses?'

'Venus, your Grace.' A full frown now lingered on his forehead.

'You let her take Venus?'

'I offered her the choice, but she was most insistent. The stray dog went with her, your Grace, and I had the impression she hoped to meet you on the way.'

Tay scanned the hills behind Alderworth and the pathways to the front.

'What time did she leave?'

'Two hours ago, your Grace.'

'Saddle Exeter for me then, and see to Hades. I will be back in fifteen minutes ready to leave.' Dismounting, he took his leather satchel and hurried inside.

Mrs Berwick was in the kitchen when he found her and up to her elbows in flour.

Tay tried to temper his worry so as not to disturb his housekeeper, but he could hear it in his voice nevertheless as he asked his question.

'Did the Duchess tell you where she was going riding today, Mrs Berwick?'

'Towards the village,' the other answered quickly. 'I gave her the directions for the pathway you would take home and she rode out to meet you.'

A whining at the door stopped him and the dog came in, panting from its exertion. Relief budded for the stable hand had said Lucinda had left with this animal, so perhaps she had already returned. The arrival of the same lad a second later put paid to such a hope.

'Her Grace is still not back, your Grace. The dog came a few minutes ago and I thought she would follow. But nothing…'

Mrs Berwick was now wiping her hands off, a look of alarm spreading across her face. 'The weather is changing, your Grace. I think it will rain soon.'

'What was my wife wearing?'

'Her riding jacket and skirt. They looked both serviceable and warm.'

Almost three hours since anyone had seen Lucinda after she had left. Kneeling down, Tay lifted the front paws of the dog and saw the telltale red dirt of the hills to the east on his feet. He had not crossed a river then or the silt would have been washed away. The choices narrowed.

Venus was not an easy mount and the terrain became hillier past the track into the village. Other more sinister thoughts followed. Had Lucinda fallen and knocked her head? He distractedly swiped away his hair. The Wellingham physician had been most explicit about the consequences of such a mishap.

Half an hour later Tay rode across the land to the east calling Lucinda's name. Six Alderworth servants fanned out on horses all around him doing the same and at every pathway that dissected the main trail he sent a man off to see if she might have branched off. Forty minutes and then fifty went past, with not a stirring of anything untoward.

His hands gripped the leather reins as the thought of not finding her consumed him. He seldom panicked, yet here he was allowing ideas to come that took him to the edge of it.

If she had hit her head somehow… The warnings that Posy Tompkins had spoken of in the park had been specific. Even a little knock might do it…

His wife's soft honesty, her smell, the way she smiled at him and stood by him. The colour of her hair falling across his body, pale against the dark, a perfect match. He could not have just found her to lose her again. The dog ran next to him, easily stretching to the pace of his horse, as one by one the miles were swallowed up.

She was shivering and even that small movement dislodged dirt from the spaces between the timber, hurling them down the steep sides of the hole where they fell into water.

Fifteen feet, she reasoned.

Two hours at least since she had been here, the sky above darkened with rain. Her head ached with the fall.

'Please, God, don't let it end like this,' she prayed and then found herself shouting Taylen's name, as loud as she could manage again and again into the silence.

A spider startled her as it jumped on to her riding jacket. She had always hated insects, but as this one with its tiny spiky legs tiptoed up her sleeve, she felt strangely aligned with it, both of them down a hole in the cold and far from safety. She watched as it crossed to a leaf further away towards the light.

'Go well,' she whispered and watched as it spun a web and swung up to another twig and then another. If only she might do the same, she thought, but her hand could not reach the branch above and the lip of the well on the other side was just too far away with skirts to hinder her.

Her throat was scratchy from shouting and her only hope of rescue lay in Dog. *Please let him have gone back to Alderworth,* she prayed. *Please let him bring help.* Her husband would come, she knew he would, and surely at the house the alarm must have already been raised.

But what if he did not come by dark? The thought crept into panic, stuck down here amongst what was left of the old tree roots. What would crawl out when the sun set and the moon rose and the cold of the night became apparent?

Again she shook away such thoughts. She was a Wellingham and she was strong. A little dark and cold could not hurt her and spiders did not bite.

She would sing, that is what she would do. She would sing and sing until they came, with her rusty voice and her lack of tune and her spirits would be raised. Sound would echo from the hollow stone and if Taylen was somewhere nearby he must surely hear it.

A sea shanty he remembered on the ship back from the Americas rang out around the small glade that Tay had followed Dog down to and he tilted his head to ascertain the exact direction.

Oh Blow the man down bullies, blow the man down,
Way, hey, blow the man down…

Lucinda. She was alive. He did not question the pure ache of relief as he dismounted and ran to an old disused well on the side of a hill.

Not wishing to scare her by suddenly appearing, he chanted the next line of the words back to her loudly.

A pretty young damsel I chanced for to meet…

The only sound then was that of sobbing, heart-broken wailing that had him lying across the edge of the opening.

When he looked down fear caught in his throat.

His wife was positioned precariously and the only thing allowing her any purchase was an old rotten tree that had fallen over, creating a makeshift ledge.

Nothing looked stable or safe.

'I think the bough beneath me will break if you come down here,' she said, her voice strained and hoarse as she tried to contain her crying. Even as she said it more dirt dribbled down the wall to be lost in the darkness of the bottom. A splash told Tay that water lay below. 'There are spiders here, too. At first I did not mind them, but now...' She stopped, giving the impression she had made herself do so.

'Stay very still, then. Don't move at all.' He glanced around for something to tie a rope to and found it in the trunk of another tree.

'No. If you fall...'

'Then we both go,' he replied, and across the rain and the dirt and in the space of eight feet their eyes caught, saying things to each other that they had not been brave enough to voice as yet.

'Is she your mistress?' Her quiet words were lost in worry.

'Who?'

'The woman I saw you with in the downstairs parlour?'

'Elizabeth Montcrieff. She was Lance's wife, my

partner in the gold mine in Georgia. I have been helping her financially.'

'But the ring you were wearing was on her wedding finger?'

'Because it once belonged to her husband and I
gave it back to her. That was all.' Her chin wobbled
and he saw her swallow, but another falling piece of
the ledge brought them back to the present danger.
'Don't move while I get the rope and push yourself
to the very back so that I can come down to you.'
The dog ran in circles around the top of the well,
barking wildly.

A moment later he had the lifeline fastened and
started to climb down the side of the drop. When he
reached Lucinda he simply laid his arms about her
and held her close. She was cold, her teeth were chat-
tering and her hair was plastered to her head with
the rain. It felt so good to hold her and cast away all
the nightmare thoughts he had had on the ride here.

'It will be all right, sweetheart. Here, grab the
rope and I will push you up.'

He took both her hands and guided them about the
thick plait of jute. 'Don't look down. As I push you
need to pull as hard as you can and try to scramble up
on the rope. When you get to the top, find the tufts of
grass and heave yourself over. Do you understand?'

She nodded.

'Are you ready?'

She nodded again.

Making a stirrup with his hands, he got her to

place her boot upon it before bringing it up as far as he could go. 'Can you see the edge?'

He felt her flurry of movement though he could not look up, his face jammed against the earth and his breathing heavy. Then the weight was gone, her boots disappearing as she levered herself across the mouth of the hole, a few errant stones coming down upon him and stinging his back.

She was safe. Lucinda was safe. He thanked the Lord for her deliverance just as the ledge crumbled away completely and he disappeared into the blackness of space.

Chapter Fifteen

Taylen was gone. The rumble of earth had taken him to the bottom, the tree he was jammed in against disappeared with him, leaving only emptiness where a second before he had stood.

There was no reality to it, no recognition of the horror of it all, only an aching searing loss that had Lucinda lying down on the grass and screaming out his name.

She could just make him out at the bottom of the hole, partly buried beneath a pile of rocks and dirt, his head turned downwards. Thankfully the width of the old tree had missed landing on him and lay at an angle to one side. Grabbing the rope, she measured the full length of it and determined it finished a few yards from the bottom. Could she get down there or would she dislodge more of the crumbling walls and damage him further? The rain solved the question completely as she saw the water running in a steady stream. He would drown if she waited too long.

Removing her stockings and boots, she tied hooped knots all the way along the stem of the rope in the way her brothers had shown her how to do so many times in her youth. Coiling the rest of the line, she then threw it over the edge, watching as it swung heavily against the side of the well. Would it hold? The tree Taylen had fastened it around had not moved at all and the anchor looked well fashioned. Fear made her sweat, the close cloying air in the hole would be even worse at the bottom and she could not see how she might be able to climb out carrying him. She would be stuck there again until help came.

Swallowing away panic, she took a deep breath before making two good tight fists and levering herself over the side, the knots and their hoops allowing both her fingers and toes a good grip as she descended.

It was easier than she thought and within a few moments she was at the bottom of her lifeline. It was a few feet short and, letting it slip from her hands, she dropped the rest of the way to land on her feet to one side of Taylen, the mud slithering between her toes and the water icy cold.

He was still alive when she touched him, still breathing as she sat to take his head carefully upon her lap, away from the water.

'Please, please be safe,' she whispered, the echo of it hollow in the depth of the earth. Blood dribbled down his face from a cut on his brow and there was a large swelling at the crown of his head. Reaching for the hem of her riding skirt, she wiped at his cheeks, the red and brown of blood and mud strangely mixed, and his skin pale beneath their hues.

Her brothers had bought her a gift of inestimable value, a man she could respect and admire and adore—a man who had risked his life to save hers and who now lay unconscious as payment for his valour.

Already the sun had fallen, daylight leached from dusk, the long shadow of night upon them. Holding him closer, she tried to impart some of her warmth into his cold, her fingers tracing the shape of him in the darkness.

He was hers and she would protect him. At Alderworth now the alarm would surely have been raised and help would be coming.

The sounds of others came quietly at first and then more loudly, the length of rope trailing above twitching and raised. She could see nothing now, the black complete.

Then there were more voices, men's voices. She recognised some of the tones of the Alderworth servants as another line dropped down beside her. A thicker rope this time and longer.

When a figure came from out of the gloom she could only watch, scared to move in case she hurt Taylen further.

A tinder flared and then there was light, a face outlined by the flame. He pulled three times on the rope and another one dropped, a man she did not recognise at all on the end of it. In his hands was a long roll of heavy calico, the ends tied to folded poles of wood.

'Briggs, your Grace. The dog led us here. Has he woken at all?'

She shook her head in answer.

'The doctor has been summoned and will be at the house by the time we are back with him.'

Laying the fabric of the stretcher to one side, they pulled the contraption into a narrow bed. The mud and water had soaked through the canvas even before they lifted Taylen slowly on to it. The pain must have leaked into his unconscious mind for he groaned, the ache in his voice making Lucinda grimace.

'Be careful,' she pleaded as the stretcher was hoisted, one foot up from the ground and then two, both men steadying an end each as they all rose, the eerie shadows of the torches showing up broken patches of the sheer earthen walls.

She was the only one left down here now, and she got to her feet unsteadily after such a long time sitting, the stretcher disappearing over the top of the lip in a calm and easy way.

Safety. Lucinda could almost taste the relief of it. The dog was barking and more lights above took away the gloom. She could make out the flares against the black sky as another figure descended.

Briggs again and holding the rope she had fashioned into foot and finger holds out to her.

'I will come up beside you, your Grace. Just hold on and they will pull you up.'

A moment later jostling hands helped her over the top and she was once again standing in open air, the huge blackness of sky above her, a few stars twinkling through the gaps in the clouds.

Taylen lay motionless, his cheeks pale and the dark runnels of dried blood powdered on his temple. He barely seemed alive, though when Lucinda laid her hand against his he tried to turn and say something. His green eyes were lost in the swollen bruising.

'You are safe now,' she said. 'There will be no more pain, I promise.' As if he understood his eyes closed of their own accord and he breathed out, heavily.

The blankets covering him were thick and warm and Lucinda felt someone place another one across her shoulders. When a cart was drawn into place a few yards away she watched as more blankets were laid down on the floor as a cushion to transport her husband back to Alderworth.

Swan the dog crawled in beside him.

'The Duke will need complete rest and quiet,' the doctor proclaimed as he regarded Taylen a few hours later. 'He has had a nasty knock to his head and concussion has resulted. From my experience with similar cases it may be a week or so until he comes to his senses, for Briggs told me it was at least twelve feet to the bottom of the well.'

The Ellesmere physician stood to one side of the bed as he stated his findings, a passionless man with little in the way of a comforting bedside manner.

'But he will recover?' Lucinda asked the question with trepidation, for Taylen was looking worse and worse as the hours marched on.

'The brain has its own peculiar timings and reasons to stay inactive; some people come back to consciousness very quickly, others languish on the netherworld for weeks or months or even years. Some stay there for ever. It is God's will. Talk to him. Tell him all the news of the house. There is a new school of thought gaining traction that says those in a deep coma are none the less aware of things about them if they have a constant source of translation from a loved one.'

A loved one? Did she qualify as that or would any interaction between them make him even worse?

'If you need me in what is left of the night, send a messenger. Otherwise I will return tomorrow afternoon to see how my patient is progressing.'

Then he was gone, Taylen lying still and Mrs Berwick fussing about with the sheets at his side.

'Are you certain you do not wish me to stay, your Grace?'

Lucinda shook her head, not trusting herself to speak and when the woman finally took her leave she sat on a chair beside her husband and reached for his hand. The nail on his right thumb had been pulled off and there were cuts across the fingers. 'If I could heal you, my darling, I would,' she murmured, tucking the blanket in further and dousing the candles so that only one still blazed, protected by a glass cover as a precaution against fire.

She watched him as the sun appeared above the hills that she held no name for, the horizon aglow with pink and yellow. She watched the rise and fall of his breath, too, and the pulse in his throat where the stubble of a twelve-hour growth darkened his skin.

His chest was bare and she could just make out the tail end of the scars by his neck where the marks had curved around from his back and licked at the sensitive folds of his throat.

Hurt by life and by his family, and then censured by society and tossed out of England all because of her lies. And all the time he had stood up to her brothers with the knowledge of what he had not done. Halsey, too. The broken ribs and the ruined face. Nobody had ever believed in him and loved him as they should have.

Nobody until now. Her grip tightened.

'I love you, Taylen. I love you so much that it hurts.' She hated the tears that were gathering in her eyes. 'If you die I don't know what I will do because there is nobody else who understands me, who makes me feel…perfect.'

Not flawed, not foolish, not merely pretty, but beautiful and strong and completely herself. Finally after all these years she knew what she had been missing, a friend, a lover, a man who might sacrifice his life to save her own.

Anger came next and she shook his hand before holding it to her lips. 'Don't you dare leave me, Taylen, because if you do I will kill you, I swear that I will…'

'Water?' The voice came croaky and deep as dark-green eyes found hers, dazed with the strong painkillers. She could not quite believe that he was conscious.

'You can hear me?'

He nodded. 'You were…threatening me.'

'And loving you.' She had to say it, had to make him understand.

'That, too.' The creases around his eyes deepened.

'For ever. I will love you for ever.' She did not try to stop the tears now as they fell in runnels down her cheeks.

Tipping his head, she offered him a drink of boiled water from a jug, careful to give only small sips in the way that the doctor had directed.

Pain scrawled deep lines into his face and he grimaced as he tried to move.

'You have a bad bump to the head and your ankle is sprained. The doctor says you are to stay very still. He will be pleased to know you have woken.'

'How…long?'

'Just a few hours. It is five o'clock in the morning and they brought you to Alderworth last night after eleven.'

Reaching for her hand, he held on.

'Don't go.'

Before she could even answer he had fallen back to sleep.

Everything hurt. His head and his eyes and his neck. He had a tight bandage wound around the top of his forehead and a flickering light had been left beside him.

Lucinda—his last moments of seeing her safe, climbing up the rope from the well at the bottom of the Thompson's Ranges. She had spoken to him some time later in the cold and the mud and then again somewhere else.

Here. His bedroom. A small hand entwined in his own. Warmth and hope and safety, her breathing even and deep beside him and the moon waning towards the dawn. Home. With his wife. Closing his eyes again, he fell asleep.

Asher Wellingham was there when he next woke up, stretched out on a chair, his long legs before him. Lucinda had gone. He felt around for her with the hand that she had held and found the bed empty.

It was almost noon because the sun was high and the shadows at the window folded down on to one another. The blue openness of sky through the drawn curtains hurt his eyes with its brightness.

'You saved Lucy and put your own life at risk. I want to thank you for that. If you had not come when you did…' He stopped, regrouping emotion before beginning again.

Seeing him awake, Asher spoke, as if his message was urgent. 'Lucinda has told us that she was mistaken about her allegations of intimacy with you at Alderworth three years ago. We had you thrown out of England on a lie, Alderworth, and you would have good reason to hate us.'

All these words at once, Tay thought, tumbling into the air around him. Where was his wife? He wanted her back.

'Lucinda?'

'She has slept beside you for the past three nights since the accident. We all thought it was time she looked after herself and took a break, though I should imagine she will be back before the clock strikes the next part of the hour. It seems she cannot stay away.'

Exhaustion hammered at Tay like a mallet and he let his eyes close.

The next time he awoke it was night and Lucinda was there, watching him.

'Welcome back.' Her smile was shy and her hair was loose, dancing in pale waves across her shoulders and down her back.

'Beautiful.' And she was, in every single way that he might imagine.

'Thank you for saving me, Taylen.' Her fingers traced the lines of a scratch across the back of his hand as though measuring the hurt. 'If you had not come…'

He stopped her. 'But I did.'

Tonight the world was sharper, less hazy. He could even lift his head from the pillow and it did not ache.

'How many days?'

'Four.'

He brought up his free hand to feel the bandage.

Memories. After Rouen. A small child without a hope in hell of protecting himself.

Lucinda knew everything hidden and still loved him?

A bunch of wildflowers sat in a vase opposite the bed, and for the first time ever the bile did not rise up in Tay's throat as he thought of his uncle. It was over, finished, and there was all of the future to look forward to. The peace of it made him smile as he spoke. 'You look happy.'

'I am. With you here next to me and a whole night of just us. Ashe also sat with you each time that I did not. Taris came, too, and Cristo. They all hope you can forgive them.'

This time he laughed. 'Forgive them for forcing you upon me? Forgive them for making my life… whole?'

Catching her hand, he brought it to his lips and

noticed an injury on the top of her knuckles from the fall. Further up on her wrist an older scar from the carriage accident lingered. He wanted to wrap her in his arms and keep her close.

When she lay down beside him to sleep he knew that he would never be lonely again.

They were all in the Alderworth dining room at the end of dinner, celebrating the first time that Taylen had been able to come downstairs unaided.

A week since he had fallen down the well. Lucinda thought it seemed like a lifetime ago.

Everyone was present, her brothers and their wives and Posy.

Cristo made certain that a comfortable chair was angled in the best way for Tay to sit in and Asher got him a drink. It was strange to see her brothers fussing over a man they had hated not so very long ago.

When Taris raised his glass he gave a toast. 'Here is to you, Taylen, and a warm welcome to our family. The beginning may not have been exactly comfortable, but we have many years now to make up for it.'

Tay smiled and took Lucinda's hand. 'Without your…help—' he gave the word the inflection of a question and everybody laughed '—I may not have found my wife.' He raised his own glass now and looked directly at her. 'To you, Lucinda, and to family.'

His green eyes brimmed with a happiness that softened the lines in his face. To Lucinda he looked the most beautiful man in the world, her man, and a husband who made her feel strong and real.

Intrinsically flawed? No, she felt far, far from that.

'To life and to laughter,' she toasted in return and looked around the table at the smiling faces as she held up her glass.

Happiness was a feeling that was almost physical. Emerald's jade talisman was warm in her palm and she knew for certain that she would ask Emerald if she could give it to Posy, who sat next to her with a look on her face that she thought might have been her own a few months back.

An observer of life, but wanting so much more.

'Has your memory returned fully yet, Lucy?' Beatrice asked the question.

'It hasn't. But there are new memories now which have replaced those old ones.'

'Then let us drink to that.' Cristo stood and poured fresh brandy into all the glasses. 'But be warned, Duke, once a Wellingham, always a Wellingham. Eight of us now and that is not counting any of the children.'

Lucinda's eyes met her husband's. Children. How she hoped that the time would come when she held the heir of Ellesmere safely in her arms.

Chapter Sixteen

London—three months later.

Tay had always hated these big society events for all of the falseness and the inherent censure within them. As the Duke of Alderworth he had been invited because of his title, but the *ton* had tiptoed around him, feared him, he supposed, and worried about what he might do or say next, every new and over-exaggerated myth that had built up around him adding to their trepidation.

An outsider. A Duke asked because it was harder to leave him out, such a slight a reminder of how far the Alderworth star had indeed fallen. Oh, granted, there were those amongst the *ton* who would gravitate to him, but they were often men he felt no true communion with or else young bucks satisfying their first urges to kick the traces and to irritate their more-than-disapproving families.

But tonight with the lights of the chandeliers full upon him and a dozen of the Wellinghams around him it was different. Every eye in the place might be turned towards their party, but the usual alarm that prickled inside him on entering such a salon was missing.

Safety. Belonging. The feel of his wife's hand tucked through the crook of his arm and her oldest brother beside him.

'A smile might persuade those who are here to criticise you to do otherwise, Tay.'

'You think it that easy?' Months of getting to know Asher Wellingham had brought them together as friends.

'The *ton* revolves around a large measure of deceit. Surely you have learned at least that?'

Such an answer did make it easy to smile, to simply laugh at all the implied deceit and make use of it. Taylen saw Taris smile, too, his wife, Beatrice-Maude, beside him in the company of Cristo, Emerald and Eleanor. Asher's friend, Jack Henshaw, also lingered amongst them, Posy Tompkins on his arm and dressed in the most absurdly expensive gown, the diamonds on the cloth glittering in the light. The plain jade pendant she had around her throat seemed very out of place in the ensemble and Tay remembered seeing the piece around Lucinda's neck and wondered.

Altogether they made up a high-ranking and prominent group and although the power of money and title was behind them, it was something much more than that again that made Tay's heart swell with pride.

Respect was something he was not used to, but it came tonight in waves from those who watched them, the consequence, he supposed, of the years of good works and care of others the Wellinghams had been involved in. And he belonged, not in the game room amongst the card sharps and the drunken care-for-nothings, but here in the bosom of the protective custody of the Carisbrooks. One of them. For ever.

His hand tightened on his wife's. 'Can I reserve every single dance, sweetheart?'

'I have already pencilled you in, Tay.'

In a light gold dress Lucinda looked unmatchable, her hair wound into curls and the *décolletage* on her dress showing off the creamy skin of her breasts.

'Should your bodice be quite so revealing?'

She simply laughed. 'This from a man who insists I come naked to bed every night?'

'There it is only us, but here…' He looked around. A good percentage of the men in the room had their eyes fastened upon his wife and he knew exactly why. It was the joy that seemed to well up in Lucinda like a fountain, spilling around her as laughter and honesty and delight. And there was something else that only he was privy to, a wild and wonderful secret that had not yet been told to anyone, save him.

They would have a child in less than six months,

and there had been no payment except for love involved in its conception.

His whole being filled with a feeling that almost frightened him with its intensity and yet when he looked at Taris and Ashe and Cristo he saw the same desperation in their eyes, too. Men made whole by their women and astonished by the fact over and over again.

'How many hours until we can be back in our bedchamber?' he whispered and saw the flush of pleasure stain her cheeks. God, he loved her puritanical bent because it was so much fun dismantling it every single night.

'Five waltzes at least, Duke,' she replied, knowing how he enjoyed holding her close to feel the slight swell of her stomach between them. Three months along. The newest Ellesmere. Another Wellingham. A cousin for all the numerous children who ran and laughed in the great estates of Falder and Beaconsfield and Graveson. Another belonging. More protection. A tight circle of safe-keeping.

Like an onion, he thought, and Lucinda was his very centre.

A soulmate. He had never expected one, never believed that after all he had been through he might find such paradise.

Tripping as he walked, he clutched at the stick he needed to use now, a reminder not of his infirmity, but of their survival.

Asher's arm came out and steadied him. 'If you get tired, we can go home.'

Tay knew Asher hated these large gatherings and smiled at the hope in his voice. 'I have promised your sister that I will dance with her.'

'You feel up to it?'

'My balance is getting better with each passing week. Doctor Cameron said that soon there will be only a little of the vertigo left.'

'A lucky escape. It could have been so much worse.'

'Lucinda could have fallen instead of me.' Taylen had relived this horror during so many nights that the dread of it was like a familiar stranger walking with him.

'No, I meant for you, Tay. You could have died.' Amber eyes looked grave.

'But instead I found everything I was looking for.' He gestured to Lucinda and to the Wellingham family all about him.

'And as Cris said, once we claim someone we keep them for ever.' Taris added this from behind, and laughter accompanied the group as they walked on to the overcrowded dance floor.

A few hours later Lucinda and Tay lay in bed with moonbeams across their bodies and the winds off Hyde Park making the trees sway as shadows on their walls. Swan the dog lay in his own bed of fur by the window, tucked into sleep. He accompanied them everywhere now, his fearful demeanour changed to one of contentment.

'I love you,' Lucinda said softly to her husband, her fingers moving across the skin of his chest and feeling his heartbeat strong and even.

'And I love you back,' he replied, the smile in his voice bringing her in further. It was colder tonight and he always felt so very warm. 'When I found you at the Croxleys' ball and offered you money for a legitimate Ellesmere heir, I did not realise that it was my heart I was giving away instead.' He stilled her hand. 'You have it all, Lucinda, every piece of my love and if anything was to happen to you…'

'It won't.' She turned over and lay across him, his face within the veil of her hair and his worry vanished to be replaced by a look that simply took her breath away.

'That first time when you came to my room at Alderworth I thought…' He stopped and swallowed. 'I thought that you might be the one to save me and I was right, sweetheart.'

'We saved each other, Taylen, and this child shall be the beginning of a whole new dynasty of Ellesmeres.'

Turning her beneath him, his lips came down across her own, all the magic that she had felt from the very first second of meeting him beginning over again.

* * * * *

REQUEST YOUR FREE BOOKS!

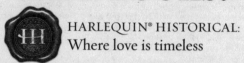

HARLEQUIN® HISTORICAL:
Where love is timeless

2 FREE NOVELS PLUS 2 FREE GIFTS!

YES! Please send me 2 FREE Harlequin® Historical novels and my 2 FREE gifts (gifts are worth about $10). After receiving them, if I don't wish to receive any more books, I can return the shipping statement marked "cancel." If I don't cancel, I will receive 6 brand-new novels every month and be billed just $5.19 per book in the U.S. or $5.74 per book in Canada. That's a savings of at least 17% off the cover price! It's quite a bargain! Shipping and handling is just 50¢ per book in the U.S. and 75¢ per book in Canada.* I understand that accepting the 2 free books and gifts places me under no obligation to buy anything. I can always return a shipment and cancel at any time. Even if I never buy another book, the two free books and gifts are mine to keep forever.

246/349 HDN FVQK

Name	(PLEASE PRINT)	

Address		Apt. #

City	State/Prov.	Zip/Postal Code

Signature (if under 18, a parent or guardian must sign)

Mail to the **Harlequin® Reader Service:**
IN U.S.A.: P.O. Box 1867, Buffalo, NY 14240-1867
IN CANADA: P.O. Box 609, Fort Erie, Ontario L2A 5X3

Want to try two free books from another line?
Call 1-800-873-8635 or visit www.ReaderService.com.

* Terms and prices subject to change without notice. Prices do not include applicable taxes. Sales tax applicable in N.Y. Canadian residents will be charged applicable taxes. Offer not valid in Quebec. This offer is limited to one order per household. Not valid for current subscribers to Harlequin Historical books. All orders subject to credit approval. Credit or debit balances in a customer's account(s) may be offset by any other outstanding balance owed by or to the customer. Please allow 4 to 6 weeks for delivery. Offer available while quantities last.

Your Privacy—The Harlequin® Reader Service is committed to protecting your privacy. Our Privacy Policy is available online at www.ReaderService.com or upon request from the Harlequin Reader Service.

We make a portion of our mailing list available to reputable third parties that offer products we believe may interest you. If you prefer that we not exchange your name with third parties, or if you wish to clarify or modify your communication preferences, please visit us at www.ReaderService.com/consumerschoice or write to us at Harlequin Reader Service Preference Service, P.O. Box 9062, Buffalo, NY 14269. Include your complete name and address.

HH13

SPECIAL EXCERPT FROM

HARLEQUIN® HISTORICAL

*Christine Merrill wraps a sensual haze of
desire around you with her brilliant new novel
THE GREATEST OF SINS,
available May 2013.*

"This is what I want," he whispered, his breath in her ear even hotter than his kiss. "And it has nothing to do with a romantic declaration, or a marriage. I want to have you, right now, here in the garden, naked like Eve. I want to use you for my pleasure, without a thought to what is right or good. I want what I want, and I do not care if it destroys us both. That is why I left six years ago. And that is why I must leave now."

And then he pushed her away, out of his lap and onto the bench. She could feel the cold night air against her exposed breasts, and the constriction of the bodice pulled low under them.

"Compose yourself. And then go back into the house and find your betrothed." His voice was cold and passionless. "Marry St. Aldric, Evie. He will care for you. I cannot." He stood then and walked away.

She tugged the bodice back into place and laid a hand against her cheek, waiting for the blush to subside. If she sat here awhile longer, she would be as cold as he was, but not as emotionless. She was angry.

Sam Hastings was all she had ever wanted. She had followed him here like a fool, only to be refused again. He had brought her to the brink of fulfillment. And then left.

Did he not realize that she might have taken some pleasure in the act that he found so base and unworthy? Her body still seethed with desire. It was as if she was waiting for some gift that only Sam could give her. He had shown it to her, held it close and then snatched it away at the last minute.

It would not happen again. Tonight, she would make her choice once and for all. She would go to another man, and she would never turn back.

Don't miss this sensational new
Regency duet from Christine Merrill
THE SINNER AND THE SAINT
Brothers separated at birth, brought together by scandal.

From the birth of a secret to the death of a lie, two brothers have been torn apart. While the duke behaves like a saint, the doctor believes himself a sinner. And only a scandal can bring them back together.
THE GREATEST OF SINS
May 2013

Look for the second in the duet,
Coming soon

HARLEQUIN® HISTORICAL:
Where love is timeless

ON THE FRONTIER OF A NEW LIFE...

Tired and hungry after two days of traveling, Susanna Hopkins is just about at the end of her tether when her train finally arrives in Cheyenne. She's bound for a new life in a western garrison town. Then she discovers she doesn't even have enough money to pay for the stagecoach! Luckily for her, the compassionate Major Joseph Randolph is heading in the same direction.

As a military surgeon, Joe is used to keeping his professional distance. But despite Susanna's understated beauty, he's drawn to this woman who carries loss and pain equal to his own and has a heart which is just as hesitant and wary....

Look for

Her Hesitant Heart
by Carla Kelly in May 2013.

Available wherever books are sold.

HH29375

HARLEQUIN® HISTORICAL:
Where love is timeless

THE SECRET LIFE OF MISS PHYLLIDA HURST

Having survived the scandal of her birth with courage
and determination, the beautiful Phyllida has reached a
precarious balance within the *ton*. And in just one moment
Ashe Herriard, Viscount Clere, blows her world and her
carefully made plans to pieces.

Brought up in vibrant Calcutta, Ashe is disdainful of polite
London society, but something about Phyllida intrigues him.
There's a mystery surrounding her. A promise of secrets and a
hint of scandal—more than enough to entice him!

Look for

Tarnished Amongst The Ton

by Louise Allen in May 2013.

Available wherever books are sold.

HARLEQUIN® HISTORICAL:
Where love is timeless

BEAUTY IS IN THE EYE OF THE BEHOLDER

Considered the plain, *clever* one in her family, Lady Cressida
Armstrong knows her father has given up on her ever marrying.
But who needs a husband when science is the only thing to set
Cressie's pulse racing?

Disillusioned artist Giovanni di Matteo is setting the *ton* abuzz
with his expertly executed portraits. Once, his art was inspired;
now it's only technique. Until he meets Cressie....

Challenging, intelligent and yet insecure, Cressie is the
one whose face and body he dreams of capturing on canvas.
In the enclosed, intimate world of his studio, Giovanni
rediscovers his passion as he awakens hers.

Look for

The Beauty Within

by Marguerite Kaye in May 2013.

Available wherever books are sold.